A BRU

"Ready for a [swim]?" [Kirk]
took Melissa's ha[nd and]
she felt a tingle [...]

Being with Kirk was like a dream—and she wanted to enjoy every minute of it. Suddenly Melissa felt as if she'd burst if she stayed quiet one second longer. She hopped up from her towel. "Race you to the water!" she called out as she ran across the hot sand.

The water was cool, but Melissa plunged in anyway and swam underwater.

"It's perfect," she said with a sigh. She hadn't felt so happy and relaxed in ages.

Kirk joined her and they floated on their backs side by side, staring at the sky. "A perfect day— and the perfect girl to spend it with," Kirk added before he dove underwater. Melissa stared after him, his words ringing in her ears. *Me? Kirk Gardener thinks I'm the perfect girl?* This had to be the happiest day of her life!

But suddenly a wave of doubt washed over her. What about the night before? What about being wrapped in Matt's strong arms and staring into his warm, sparkling eyes?

Sweet Dreams

A BRUSH WITH LOVE
Stephanie St. Pierre

BANTAM BOOKS
NEW YORK · TORONTO · LONDON · SYDNEY · AUCKLAND

RL 6, IL age 11 and up

A BRUSH WITH LOVE
A Bantam Book / January 1991

For Scott

Chapter One

"Try not to look so glum," Jill said with a laugh as she hugged Melissa goodbye. "After all, it's only for three weeks."

"Have a great time," Melissa said, pushing some stray wisps of sun-streaked brown hair out of her eyes and flipping her braid back over her shoulder. "Just please write to me at least *once*." Melissa opened her car door and reached for something on the front seat. "Maybe this will help," she said. Her hazel eyes sparkled with laughter as she gave the notepad to Jill.

"I can't believe you still have this!" Jill cried, looking at the dancing bears in the margin of the purple notepad. Jill had given the writing paper to Melissa the summer after fifth grade when Melissa went away to camp.

"I found it when I was cleaning out my desk the other day," Melissa said. "Remember how many letters we wrote that summer?"

"About a million, I think." Jill smoothed her red curls into a tiny ponytail as she spoke, then let them go. "I'll never forget how exciting it was when one of those purple envelopes appeared in the mailbox."

"Yeah, talk about exciting!" Melissa laughed. " 'Dear Jill, how are you? I am fine. Today we went horseback riding and played tennis. Write back soon. Love, Melissa.' "

"I promise my letters will be more interesting than that!" Jill said emphatically.

Melissa frowned. "I doubt I'll have much of anything to say. Between work and helping out at home, I don't think there will be time for much else. And with you and Amy gone, nothing fun will happen. I mean, what's going to happen to just *me*?"

Jill was on her way to tennis camp and Melissa's other best friend, Amy, was on vacation in the mountains with her family. Neither would be back until the day before they started their junior year at Monroe High.

"Speaking of work," Jill said. "You'd better get going. You're already late."

"Talk about dying of boredom," Melissa groaned,

thinking of the flower shop where she worked. "I can't wait to be through with this job. If I never smell another rose, it will be too soon." The girls hugged again and Melissa slid behind the wheel and started the car.

"Bye!" Jill waved for a minute, then turned and ran inside to finish packing.

Melissa knew how excited Jill was about leaving, even if it did mean abandoning her best friend for three weeks. Getting into tennis camp was a terrific accomplishment—only the best athletes in Connecticut had been accepted, and Jill had worked hard all year to get in. Melissa felt proud of her friend, even if she felt a little sad at being left alone.

But then if it hadn't been for her job, Melissa would have spent the whole month of August with Amy up at the lake. When Amy had invited her, Melissa had decided to quit her job and go on the trip. Unfortunately, her parents hadn't gone along with the idea. Melissa had agreed to work for Mr. Grover until school started, they'd said, and it would be irresponsible and unfair to back out on that agreement so late in the summer.

They probably were right, Melissa thought with a sigh. Mr. Grover would never have found someone to replace her at the last minute. Still, she resented staying home. It seemed like the only thing she'd done all summer was work. Her job kept her busy from nine until one, six mornings a week, and with her little brother, Timmy, away at camp, she had a long list of chores to take care of in the afternoon. What with helping with the gardening, cleaning up after dinner, and taking care of her own room and whatever little task her mother needed her to do, there wasn't a lot of time left over for anything. Melissa sulked all the way to work. When she got there, Mr. Grover frowned at her.

"You're almost an hour late," he said, scratching his round bald head.

"I'm sorry," Melissa snapped, sounding more angry than sorry. "My best friend is leaving town and . . . I guess I just lost track of the time."

She stuck her purse behind the counter and stared at a pile of African daisies that were waiting to be trimmed. As she pulled her dark green apron off its hook, she noticed three big boxes of flowers that had arrived that morning and needed to be unpacked, sorted, trimmed, and put in vases in the big glass-fronted refrigerator. She put the apron on over her white T-shirt and jeans and tied it around her slim waist. Because she was only five feet tall, the apron came down almost to her ankles, which for some reason Melissa found especially irritating today.

"Just call next time," Mr. Grover said. He didn't seem mad, but he did seem confused. Melissa was always on time, even early. "I was getting a little worried, so I tried to reach you at home. You'd better call and let your mother know you're here."

Melissa felt herself bristle. What right did he have to call her mother? Then she stopped herself. She'd been almost an hour late, *that's* what right he had. He'd probably thought she was sick or something.

"I'm sorry," she said again, meaning it this time. "I guess I'm just having a bad day."

Mr. Grover finished tying a pink-and-blue bow on a bouquet of tiny rosebuds in a white ceramic vase. Even in her bad mood Melissa had to admire how pretty it was.

"Don't worry about it," he said with a smile and pointed to the phone, which was half-hidden behind a huge vase of red and yellow snapdragons. "Now call your mother so you can get to work. I've got to go make some deliveries."

Melissa tapped her nails against the marble counter as the phone rang and rang. She was about to hang up when her mother finally picked up.

"Hi, Mom, it's me," Melissa said. "I'm at work."

"Melissa? Thank goodness you're all right. I was just about to get in the car and go looking for you. What happened?"

Now Melissa was really annoyed. Ever since Timmy had left for camp, her mother had been treating her like *she* was the nine-year-old. She couldn't go anywhere without being grilled about it later. "I stopped by Jill's to say goodbye and lost track of the time, that's all. It's no big deal, Mom."

"Well, as long as you're all right. Don't forget the painters are coming this afternoon, so please don't be late. I need you to help me move the furniture out of the way and take down the curtains before they can start on the upstairs room."

Melissa made a face at the phone and sighed. "Right, Mom. See you later."

"I love you," Mrs. Darby said with feeling.

"I love you, too, Mom," said Melissa, softening. As she hung up the phone, Melissa resolved to try not to lose her temper for the rest of the day. She was so touchy lately. Was she going crazy? Or was it normal to feel this way?

After she and Mr. Grover went over the list of things that had to be done and loaded up the van, he left to make deliveries at the hospital downtown. Melissa turned on the radio that sat on a cluttered shelf next to the cash register, then set to work trimming the daisies. It wasn't really such a bad job, Melissa thought as she worked. Arranging flowers, taking phone orders, and ringing up sales was actually sort of fun. Besides, the shop was never very busy and Mr. Grover was a pretty nice boss. Still, it could get kind of boring at times.

As Melissa finished trimming the last daisy, the phone rang. It was an order for a dozen long-stemmed red roses to be delivered to a woman who worked in the office building across the street. "Just say, 'From a secret admirer,' " the man on the other end of the phone instructed.

Melissa sighed as she wrote out the card. How romantic . . . and exciting. She carefully filled a long silver box with bright green tissue paper and ferns, then the roses. As she tied up the box with a beautiful red silk ribbon and tucked the card behind the bow, Melissa wondered if anyone would ever send *her* a dozen roses with a mysterious message. Probably not, she decided.

The only flowers she'd ever been given had come from her former boyfriend, Craig. Freshman year he'd bought her a beautiful corsage of white orchids for the Christmas dance. Melissa still had the corsage, all dried and brown now, its big pink satin bow still bright, nestled in the little plastic box it had come in. Whenever she looked at it, she thought about Craig and felt happy. He'd moved to another state at the end of the year and over time they'd lost touch, but he was her first boyfriend and would always be special.

Melissa noticed the clock above the door with a start. She'd spent half an hour daydreaming and now she'd be lucky if she finished everything before Mr. Grover came back. First she had to unpack the three new boxes of flowers, then she had four more flower arrangements to make up.

Putting together the arrangements was Melissa's favorite part of the job. She hummed and sang along with the radio as she snipped flowers and leaves and stuck them carefully into the square of green foam inside the vase. Most of the arrangements were made according to patterns in a big book, but today she had one arrangement to make up on her own. She did the others first and was happily working on the big vase of wildflowers when the bell above the door rang. Melissa was so involved in her work that she didn't look up to see who had come into the shop until she had finished placing the flower she was working with.

"Oh!" Melissa was startled to see Matt Warner, one of the cutest, most popular guys from school, staring at her from the other side of the flower arrangement.

"Hi," he said, flashing her a dazzling smile. "I need some flowers."

Melissa could feel herself blushing. "Uh, sure," she said. "I didn't mean to keep you waiting. What can I get for you?" Melissa suddenly felt very nervous. She'd had a crush on Matt Warner for as long as she could remember. So did most of her friends. But she'd never expected to actually *speak* to him. Melissa stared for a second, taking in Matt's tall, athletic frame, his tousled brown hair and sparkling blue eyes, and that incredible smile. He was undeniably a hunk.

"I need something really nice, but not too expensive," Matt said. "It's for my mother." His blue eyes twinkled brightly, as if he were laughing to himself.

How sweet! Melissa thought, smiling. *A cool guy like this buys his mom flowers.*

Melissa reminded herself to be professional. "How much can you afford to spend?" she asked seriously.

"Around ten dollars." Matt picked up some of the daisies Melissa had been working with. "How about some of these?"

"Sorry, those are for a special order. And they're pretty expensive, anyway." Melissa slipped off her stool and came around the counter. "There are a lot of nice things over here." She pointed to a small section of the big refrigerator where the flowers were stored. Matt came and stood behind her, and a chill ran up her spine. She felt very short next to him. She was wondering how tall he was—at least six feet—when suddenly he pulled on the long braid that hung down her back.

"Hey, cut it out," she said, then began to laugh. It was hard to be serious around Matt.

"Sorry." He ran his hand through his own shaggy brown hair. "I never could resist pulling girls' pigtails," he added, but he didn't look very sorry.

"It's not a pigtail," Melissa said with mock indignation. "Anyway, look at these flowers. You can pick out a few different kinds and make a nice bouquet for ten fifty." Melissa turned to go back to work on her flower arrangement.

"Wait! You have to help me," Matt pleaded.

Looking back over at him, Melissa felt her heart skip a beat. How could she say no to the gorgeous blue eyes that were staring into her own? She knew she should help Matt get the bouquet picked out quickly so that she could get back to work, but somehow she couldn't help joking around with him. After they selected a handful of flowers, she wrapped them up nicely and finished the bouquet with a bow. Then he pulled two roses out of the big vase in the refrigerator and stuck one behind her ear. Melissa blushed again. Her hazel eyes sparkled as she laughed happily.

"Tango?" he asked, holding the other rose stem between his teeth. "Ouch!"

"Watch out for the thorns," Melissa warned between giggles. Matt adjusted his rose, this time avoiding the thorns, and held his arms out to her, inviting her to dance.

"No, I can't." Melissa shook her head and tried to stifle her laughter. "Honestly, I've got to get back to work."

Matt grinned at her, then moved to the middle of the store where there was more room. He began stamping his feet and snapping his fingers over his head, all the while holding the rose between his teeth and humming something that sounded vaguely Spanish. There really was no way Melissa could work while Matt was there, and before she knew it she was tapping her feet, snapping her fingers, and humming along.

"Olé!" Matt shouted, leaping high in the air, and landing gracelessly with a loud thud. Melissa was doubled over with laughter as Matt tripped over his own feet and almost knocked into a large potted plant.

When the bell over the shop door rang, Melissa could barely control her giggling—until she saw the look on Mr. Grover's face.

"*What* is going on?" Mr. Grover demanded.

Melissa froze, feeling the bottom drop out of her stomach. But Matt calmly removed the rose from between his teeth, placed it on the counter, and gathered up the bouquet Melissa had made for his mother.

"Just picking up some flowers," he said innocently. Then he turned to Melissa and handed her $10.50. "Thanks for your help," he said. Then he was gone.

Dumbfounded, Melissa stood gaping at the money in her hand. When she looked up, Mr. Grover was scowling at her, waiting for an explanation. Suddenly she remembered the rose behind her ear. She self-consciously pulled it out and carefully laid it on the counter next to the one Matt had left behind.

"I'm sorry," she said. "He came in for some flowers and I was helping him pick them out and he just started goofing around. I guess we got a little carried away." Melissa was terribly embarrassed. There was a long, awkward silence.

"Well, no harm done, I suppose." Mr. Grover didn't sound happy. "Are the deliveries ready?"

"Uh, well . . ." Melissa wanted to crawl under the counter and hide. Why was this happening to her? "All except the big one. I was working on that when . . ." Her voice trailed away.

"Melissa, that arrangement is for a very good

client of mine. I trusted you with it because you usually do such nice work and I've never had to worry about you getting things done on time." Mr. Grover paused, obviously exasperated. "When do you think you can have it ready?"

Melissa hurried over to the vase. She'd only just begun working on it when Matt had arrived.

"I'll need at least an hour," she said, biting her lip. She knew that would put the whole delivery schedule way behind.

"Then go on and get to work," Mr. Grover said. "I'll handle the other orders and come back for the big arrangement later so we won't fall too far behind schedule."

Melissa nodded and started placing flowers in the vase while Mr. Grover loaded up the truck.

"And no high jinks while I'm gone, please," he said as he left, shaking his bald head.

After Mr. Grover left, Melissa's mind wandered back to the incident with Matt. It still seemed impossible. Matt Warner! She couldn't get over the fact that only a short while ago he'd been dancing with her. He'd smiled at her and stared into her eyes. Oh, what incredible blue eyes Matt had. Melissa wondered if she'd see him again before school started. If she did, would he remember her? Even if she didn't see him before school started, Melissa vowed to herself that when it did, she'd search the halls of Monroe High for him just to say hello. She sighed and smiled. Wait till Jill heard about this!

Melissa reminded herself that she was wasting precious time and got back to work on her flower arrangement. Still, every once in a while she giggled at the thought of Matt Warner tangoing in the flower shop.

Melissa made an extra-special effort to be sure the flowers were perfect. She was admiring her work, pleased with the way the bright pink and orange African daisies looked with the delicate blue cornflowers and snowy white Queen Anne's lace, when Mr. Grover returned.

"Good job," he said, picking up the vase. "I'll see you tomorrow, and, please . . . be on time."

Melissa promised she would be, and after cleaning up the counter, she left for home. It wasn't until she pulled into the driveway that she realized she was late, and that her mother would be waiting for her. She ran into the house. "Mom?"

"Upstairs," came a muffled voice. Melissa hurried upstairs and found her mother struggling with the heavy drapes in the master bedroom. "I could use some help," she said. From the tone of her voice, Melissa could tell that her mother was angry.

"Mom, I couldn't help it." Melissa began, holding one end of the blue velvet curtain. "I had to

14

stay late at the shop to finish up some things." Melissa felt a little guilty knowing that she'd had to stay late because she'd been goofing around instead of doing her job.

"Well, the painters are late, too," her mother sighed, "so we'll have time to get things ready before they arrive. I just didn't want them standing around with nothing to do, since I'm paying them by the hour."

Once the curtains were down in her mother's room, Melissa went to her own room and began clearing things off the windowsills and moving her things away from the walls. As she pulled her desk toward the middle of the room, she noticed a letter from Amy that must have arrived that morning.

I'll just sit for a minute and read it quickly, she thought. It turned out to be a long letter full of news. Amy had a new boyfriend! Melissa was just rereading the last paragraph, amused by the details about Amy's new love, when she heard a sharp rap on the door. She looked up, surprised.

"Melissa! You haven't done a thing!" Mrs. Darby was really furious now. "How do you expect me to do all this by myself? What is going on?"

Melissa knew her mother needed her help, but she couldn't help feeling angry. "I'm just

15

reading a letter," she said. "Can't I even read a letter?" Melissa was so mad that she got up and ran past her mother. Why was everybody giving her such a hard time today? She ran down the stairs and pushed open the screen door. A second later she crashed right into someone who was about to ring the doorbell.

"Ugh," Melissa said as she fell back onto the porch. She heard someone laughing. Why did that laugh sound so familiar? Where had she heard it before? Then she looked up and saw Matt Warner's twinkling blue eyes shining down at her.

Chapter Two

"Hey, are you all right?" Someone tall and tan and very blond reached down to help Melissa up. She couldn't see his face because the sun was behind him.

"Yeah," Melissa said, taking his hand. "Sorry, I wasn't looking where I was going." Melissa looked at Matt, who smiled back. "What are *you* doing here?" she asked.

"We're here to paint," Matt said. "How about you?"

Melissa laughed despite herself. "I live here," she said.

"You two know each other?" the other painter asked.

"She's the girl from the flower shop," Matt

17

said with a glint in his eye. "I hope your boss wasn't too mad."

"It worked out all right," Melissa said, shrugging. Now she recognized the other guy, Kirk Gardener. He was a senior like Matt and the star of the varsity soccer team.

"By the way," Matt asked, "what's your name? I'm Matt Warner and this is Kirk Gardener."

"I'm Melissa," she answered. Of course she knew who both of them were, but she decided to play things a little cool and act as if she'd never noticed them before either.

Just then Mrs. Darby appeared, looking flushed and surprised.

"I didn't realize you'd gotten here," she said to the boys. "Come in and I'll show you where to start. It's awfully late and there's a lot to do. You'll probably be here all night."

Matt and Kirk picked up their buckets and ladders and followed Mrs. Darby inside and up the stairs. Melissa's head was reeling. How could her mother have hired Matt Warner and Kirk Gardener to paint their house and not have even *told* her? Amy and Jill would be so mad that they weren't around for this. Two absolute hunks hanging around painting her house for days. Maybe even weeks! Melissa couldn't believe her luck. Maybe it wouldn't be such a boring three weeks until school started, after all! And Matt seemed to like her. Who knew where that might lead. Melissa sat down on the porch steps and began thinking about how popular she would be at school with Matt and Kirk as friends, maybe even as boyfriends! Well, she probably couldn't have *both* of them as boyfriends, but still . . .

"Melissa?" It was her mother.

"Yes, Mom," Melissa sighed. "Need any more help inside?" Melissa didn't want to fight with her mother; it just seemed to happen more and more often lately.

"No," Mrs. Darby said as she sat down on the porch steps beside Melissa. "I want to talk to you about what's been going on today. First you're late for work and worry everyone. Then you're late coming home and act as if you're being forced into slave labor because I ask you to help out a little."

"I'm sorry." Melissa stared at the steps, feeling glum. She hadn't done anything wrong; she'd only been having a little fun and gotten wrapped up in things that took her mind off her boredom. Now everyone was mad at her. It didn't seem fair.

"Honey"—Mrs. Darby put her arm around Melissa's shoulders— "I know how hard it is for you not to have Jill and Amy around, and I know you weren't pleased that Dad and I wouldn't let you go to the lake, but you're old enough now to act responsibly. If you think I'm being unfair, then tell me and maybe we can work things out. Don't just stew about everything."

"It just seems like I can't even have a little fun," Melissa complained.

"I'm sorry if I've been hard on you lately. I'll try not to overload you with chores, okay?" her mother said. Melissa nodded. "Why don't you call someone and make plans to go out tonight? You do have other friends besides Jill and Amy, you know."

"I know," said Melissa, "but . . ." She sighed again.

"Whatever you want," Mrs. Darby said. "I'm going in to start dinner. Coming?"

Melissa shook her head. "I think I'll sit out here for a while longer." Staring at the birds chasing each other around a nearby tree, she thought about Matt and Kirk again. How could she get to spend some time with them without being too obvious? Would it seem too pushy if she just went upstairs and talked to them? Probably, but what, then?

Melissa got up and went inside. As she passed the hall mirror, she stopped. Examining herself, she winced, remembering Matt's remark about pulling pigtails. He probably thought she looked like a baby. The long braid would have to go. Maybe she should just cut it off.

She pulled the elastic out of her hair and began to undo her braid. When her golden brown hair was loose, looking extra wavy from the braid, she leaned over and shook her head, letting her hair fly wildly around. Just as she whipped it back and stood up, she saw Kirk coming down the stairs.

"Wow," he said, his dark eyes wide, "you sure do have a lot of hair."

"I'm thinking of cutting it," Melissa said in her most offhand way. "It seems sort of . . . boring, you know?"

Kirk shook his head. "It isn't boring at all. Actually, I love long hair, but hardly any girls I know wear theirs long these days. You remind me of Rapunzel with all that hair."

Melissa blushed. She didn't know what to say. "Um, are you looking for something?"

"I need to use the phone to call home," Kirk said. "It looks like we're going to be here past suppertime and I want to let my mom know I'll be late."

Melissa showed Kirk to the phone and stood watching from the doorway as he dialed. She was surprised but pleased at how friendly Kirk seemed. His smile didn't have the same devilish sparkle that Matt's did, but to Melissa it seemed warmer somehow. Maybe it had something to do with Kirk's big dark brown eyes; they seemed so full of emotion. Maybe she wouldn't cut her hair, after all.

Melissa managed to get through dinner and

even to talk about being late to work without having a fight with her parents. That was a relief. Lately it seemed as if they couldn't talk enough about responsibility and living up to your commitments. Melissa thought she was pretty responsible and it rubbed her the wrong way to be criticized all the time. Even when her parents were right, she still felt annoyed with them. It was all so confusing.

While she was cleaning up the kitchen, Melissa thought about Timmy, her little brother. He was at sleep-away camp that summer for the first time. She had to admit she missed him. He usually helped her with the dishes after dinner, and he always made her laugh by telling silly jokes and stupid stories that only a nine-year-old could come up with. *Maybe Mom misses him, too,* Melissa thought. *Maybe that's why she won't leave me alone.*

When she was finished in the kitchen, Melissa went upstairs to reread her letter from Amy. She planned to sit down and write her a long letter, describing all the crazy things that had happened today—especially about meeting Matt and Kirk. When she got to her room, though, Melissa was surprised to see the two boys on ladders painting her ceiling. She thought they'd be working in her parents' room.

"Hi," Matt said. "Did you bring us some of that delicious dinner we smelled?" He was joking, but Melissa realized they must be starving; it was almost nine o'clock.

"Sorry, we ate it all." Melissa looked around her room. Everything was covered with big white sheets. She'd never find Amy's letter in the mess, but now she had a great excuse to spend some time with the guys. "Would you like some sandwiches? And maybe some lemonade?" she offered.

"That sounds great," Kirk said, running a paint-splattered hand through his hair. "That way we won't faint from hunger and thirst and mess up your room."

"You'd better not," Melissa joked. Matt still made her nervous—she'd spent so much time admiring him and talking about him with her friends that it was hard to think of him as just a regular guy. But Kirk put Melissa at ease. She felt comfortable joking around with him. "I'll be back with the food soon."

As she passed the family room, she stuck her head in the doorway. "I'm going to make some sandwiches for the painters, okay?" Melissa asked her mother.

"Oh, thank you, honey," Mrs. Darby said. "I forgot all about them."

Melissa headed to the kitchen and got out some ham and turkey, a loaf of bread, mustard, mayonnaise, some cheese, lettuce, and tomato, and started assembling a pile of sandwiches.

Then she mixed up a pitcher of lemonade and put everything on a big tray.

"Food!" Matt gasped as she entered the room. He leaped from his ladder and landed with a thump in front of Melissa. Grabbing a sandwich, he began eating as if he hadn't seen food in years.

"Hey, watch out," Melissa said with a giggle. "I almost dropped the tray."

"No problem," Kirk said as he hopped down off his own ladder with a little more grace, "he'd just eat off the floor. The guy is an animal." Kirk sat on the edge of her sheet-draped desk, then took the tray from Melissa and set it in his lap.

"Thanks," Matt said as he gulped down a tall glass of lemonade. "I feel much better now." He took another sandwich from the tray and sat on the bed, munching calmly.

It was definitely weird to see these guys sitting in her room like it was something they did every day. If she called Amy and Jill now and told them that Matt Warner and Kirk Gardener were sitting around eating sandwiches in her room, they'd think she was nuts. They'd also rush right over. *Why couldn't they be here?* Melissa thought, suddenly missing her two best friends terribly. She could just imagine the three of them kidding around with Matt and Kirk. It would be so much fun. Jill and Kirk would probably talk about sports and outgoing Amy would just talk!

Matt was on the soccer team with Kirk, too, but he was just an average player. Melissa remembered him being taken out of a game last season because he'd been making fun of the referee. The crowd had loved his clowning around, but the referee hadn't and neither had the coach. But Matt hadn't seemed to care even when he was benched for the rest of the game.

"So how did your mom like the flowers?" Melissa asked Matt.

"Oh, they did the trick," he answered. "She loved them and she said they really made up for everything." Kirk and Matt looked at each other and started to laugh.

"What did you do?" Melissa demanded, wanting to get in on the fun.

"First, you have to understand that crazy things just happen to Matt," Kirk said. Matt was too busy laughing to speak. "His mom has all these ladies over to lunch to play Scrabble every couple of weeks, and . . ." Kirk started laughing too hard to continue. Melissa was even more curious now.

"What did you do? Tell me!" She looked at Matt. He was smiling, his eyes glittering with mischief.

"I didn't exactly plan it," he explained. "It just

25

sort of happened. You see, I misread the timer . . . It was *so* funny," Matt gasped.

"What?" Melissa had to know.

"Okay," Matt said between chuckles. He took a deep breath to stop laughing. "We have this automatic sprinkler system in our yard, and it's set on a timer. My mom and her friends were sitting out there playing Scrabble, and—"

"Oh, no! You didn't turn it on?" Melissa couldn't believe he would have done that. It was funny, but it was pretty mean, too.

"You should have seen them," Kirk added. "They were screaming and running around and knocking over the tables."

"Everybody got soaked," Matt went on. Melissa couldn't help laughing, too, imagining how silly it must have looked.

"And your mother wasn't mad just because you gave her some flowers?" Melissa couldn't believe that.

"Well, it *was* an accident," Matt said. "I miss-set the timer. It was supposed to go off in the middle of the night, not the middle of the afternoon."

"Melissa!" It was Mr. Darby calling from downstairs. "Are you still up there?"

"Yes, Dad. I'll be right there." Matt and Kirk got up and started putting away their brushes and paint.

"Guess it's pretty late," Kirk said. "We'd better clean up and get going so we can come back early tomorrow. I don't want to spend every night painting."

Melissa went downstairs to talk to her parents. She was sorry that Matt and Kirk had to leave, but she did have to get up for work tomorrow and she couldn't be late.

"Why don't you sleep down here on the couch tonight," Mr. Darby said. Melissa got sheets and set up the couch as a bed. Just as she finished, she heard Matt and Kirk clomping down the stairs.

"Bye," she called from the doorway. "See you."

"Maybe I'll drop by the flower shop tomorrow," Matt said with an evil glint in his eye.

"No! Please don't," Melissa cried, laughing, but she almost hoped that he would. "I can't afford to lose my job!"

Finally they were gone, the house was quiet, and everyone got ready for bed. Melissa still couldn't find her letter from Amy or her stationery, but she was too tried to write a letter now, anyway.

What a day, Melissa thought as she snuggled under her sheet on the couch. What a crazy wonderful day.

Chapter Three

Melissa was sitting in front of a bowl of corn flakes thinking about Matt and Kirk when her mother came into the kitchen.

"You and the boys seemed to be getting along pretty well last night," Mrs. Darby said. "Do you know them from school?"

Melissa laughed a little. "They're only two of the most popular guys at Monroe, Mom. Everybody knows them." Melissa shook her head, then dug into her cereal. She still couldn't believe her mother hadn't mentioned whom she'd hired to paint the house before they'd arrived.

"Well, I'm glad they seemed to cheer you up a bit last night. It's a shame you won't be home anymore when they're working."

Melissa's spoon dropped into her bowl with a splash. "What do you mean?" she asked.

"They want to get started earlier in the day," Mrs. Darby explained as she sipped her coffee. "Yesterday they couldn't make it in the morning, but from now on they'll be working from nine until around one. So I doubt you'll be around."

"That's terrible," Melissa cried, suddenly losing her appetite. Her dreams of getting to know Matt and Kirk, of becoming friends with them, were shattered. She'd probably never see Matt or Kirk again unless she happened to run into them at school, where they wouldn't even notice she was alive. "Are you *sure* they can't come later?" Melissa wondered, trying not to sound as crushed as she felt.

"It doesn't matter to me when they come," Mrs. Darby said, seeming surprised at how upset Melissa was. "I think they've got other commitments, though."

Melissa scraped her chair back from the table and took her bowl to the sink.

"I've got to get to work," she said with a sigh as she poured milk and cereal into the sink. "Mr. Grover will go nuts if I'm late again." Melissa got her purse and walked slowly to the kitchen door.

"Goodbye, sweetheart," her mother called.

"Bye," Melissa said dully as she headed out to her car.

Though she was five minutes early, Mr. Grover was waiting impatiently for Melissa to arrive. He practically pounced on her when she walked into the store.

"Two luncheons, three dinner parties, and a country club banquet," he said, holding a long list of orders for flower arrangements under Melissa's nose. "We'll be busy today!"

"Great," Melissa said, trying to hide her sarcasm.

But Mr. Grover was oblivious to her bad mood. He bustled around the shop in a frenzy, pulling out bunches of flowers and unwinding yards of ribbon as he prepared the centerpieces for the luncheons. Melissa sighed and bit her lip. She couldn't stop stewing over the fact that at that very moment Matt and Kirk were probably in her room painting and clowning around—without her. It was too depressing.

Melissa sat on her stool at the worktable and started on an arrangement. She'd almost finished one when Mr. Grover gasped.

"What is *that*?" he asked in horror. He was staring at the arrangement Melissa had been absentmindedly working on.

Melissa looked at the small vase of flowers. "Yikes!" she cried, her eyes wide. She hadn't been paying very much attention and hadn't even realized that she'd been picking stems from a pile of withered flowers and stems that were meant for the trash. Next to it was a pile of fresh, beautiful carnations, roses, and greens. In her distracted state, she'd even gone as far as to tie a ribbon around the vase. It was almost funny, but Melissa knew Mr. Grover took flower arranging very seriously.

"Oh, I'm sorry," Melissa said as she quickly plucked out the dead stems and started over. "I guess I'm not feeling very well today. I'm having a hard time concentrating with this terrible headache." Suddenly she realized she really did have a headache.

"Maybe you should go home?" Mr. Grover suggested. He was genuinely concerned, but Melissa could see in his eyes that he hoped she would stay. There was no way he could finish all the work today by himself.

"That's okay," Melissa sighed. "I'll just take some aspirin. I'm sure I'll be fine in a few minutes." She picked up her purse and disappeared into the bathroom.

Get a hold of yourself, Melissa, she thought as she glared at her reflection in the mirror over the sink. She would have loved to be at home at least once more while Matt and Kirk were working, but she couldn't just leave Mr. Grover in the lurch. On the other hand, she couldn't afford to be so distracted that she'd make any more crazy centerpieces. She drummed her fingers against the sink as she thought. Finally she came up with a plan.

"I'm feeling better," Melissa said when she returned to the workroom. Mr. Grover seemed relieved. Melissa switched on the radio and got back to work. Now that she knew she'd see Matt and Kirk again, she didn't mind doing the arrangements at all. She even sang along with her favorite songs.

It was late by the time all the arrangements were done and loaded into the van. After cleaning up, Melissa was more than ready to go home. It was almost four. Even though she knew the guys wouldn't be there, Melissa still couldn't help racing home or being disappointed when she pulled into the driveway and didn't see Matt's car. Still, she had a plan, she reminded herself.

She went into the kitchen to make a sandwich and found a note from her mother saying she'd gone shopping. Melissa was pleased that she'd have the afternoon to herself for a change. She could write to Amy and Jill without being interrupted to do chores every five minutes. After she finished eating, Melissa went to her room to find Amy's letter and get some stationery. She was surprised to see her furniture back in place and the walls glowing with fresh yellow paint. But even better, propped up on her desk was a note—from Matt and Kirk.

"Dear Melissa," it said. "Hope you like the new paint job. Sorry you weren't around today. Nobody fed us." It was signed, "Two hungry painters."

It wasn't exactly the sort of message Melissa had hoped for, but at least they had left her a note. They had even missed her company. It was a good thing she'd decided to stay home from work tomorrow.

Amy's letter was on the desk where Melissa had left it yesterday. After rereading it, she sat down to write back, asking lots of questions about Jeremy, Amy's new boyfriend. Then she wrote about meeting Matt and Kirk. Melissa thought happily about the two gorgeous, funny guys who had suddenly appeared in her life when she'd least expected them. When she'd finished the letter to Amy, she started one to Jill, who would be especially interested to hear about Kirk. Jill always raved about what an incredible soccer player he was.

Yawning, Melissa decided the letter to Jill could wait until tomorrow. What she really wanted to do right now was take a nap. After staying up late the night before and working all day, she was exhausted. As she nestled into her pillows, she quickly felt herself falling into a delicious slumber.

Suddenly she was in the flower shop. Matt and Kirk were both there—Matt looking more tousled and wild than before with the rose between his teeth, dancing and acting crazy; Kirk, blond hair gleaming, holding a bouquet of long-stemmed roses tied with a long silver ribbon. Melissa was looking down at them from a tower that had suddenly appeared in a corner of the shop. Her long braid hung out the window and stretched toward the floor. She was dressed in a velvet gown embroidered with pearls and gold. She desperately wanted to climb out of the tower to dance with Matt, or to take the flowers that Kirk was holding out to her, but Mr. Grover stood at the base of the tower saying that she couldn't come down until she had finished arranging the flowers in her room. Melissa turned to look behind her and saw that the room was filled with a huge empty vase and thousands of flowers.

"No!" she cried in the dream, waking herself up. When she opened her eyes, she saw her mother hurrying into her room. Melissa sat up in bed and rubbed her eyes.

"Are you all right?" Mrs. Darby asked, her eyes full of concern.

"I'm fine, Mom," Melissa said groggily. "I just had a bad dream." Then she remembered her plan. "Actually, I have a really bad headache. I thought taking a nap would make it better, but I still feel pretty crummy."

Melissa's mother reached out to feel her forehead. "You don't seem to have a fever," she said. "But you have been working awfully hard lately. Maybe you should stay home tomorrow and just get some rest. Do you think Mr. Grover can manage without you?"

"Yes, I think so. Besides, I worked till four today even though I felt sick. I don't think he'd mind at all if I stayed home." The plan was going to work! Tomorrow Melissa would be home and she'd get to see Matt and Kirk. Now she just had to figure out what to do next.

"Would you like me to bring your dinner up on a tray?" Mrs. Darby asked as she got up to leave.

"No, that's okay," said Melissa with a smile. She didn't want to get carried away. "I don't feel so terrible that I can't come to the table to eat, but I don't think I'll have much of an appetite." That was true. Now that she was going to see her secret crush again, Melissa was too excited to think about food.

Despite the fact that she didn't have to work, Melissa got up early Wednesday morning. She took a long shower and spent almost an hour drying and styling her hair. When she gave it a final brush, though, Melissa had to admit her hair looked fantastic. It was golden brown, thick and wavy with a healthy sheen, and it reached just about to her waist. Usually she wore it in one long braid because it was so much simpler than having all her hair flying around, but today was special. After all, Kirk had called her Rapunzel. She remembered the look in his eyes when she'd taken her braid out the other day, and smiled. Besides, now Matt wouldn't be tempted to pull her braid and make her feel silly.

Once her hair was done, Melissa carefully applied her makeup, a pale violet eye shadow to bring out the green in her hazel eyes, a light coat of mascara, soft pink blush, and a natural-colored lip gloss. Melissa thought she looked fine without makeup, but a little extra color really made her sparkle. Satisfied that she looked as pretty as she could, Melissa went to her room to get dressed. On the way out of the bathroom she bumped into her father, who was hurrying downstairs for breakfast.

"You certainly look nice this morning," he said with a smile. "What's the occasion? I thought you were sick?" Melissa panicked. Maybe her father would insist she go to work, after all.

"Don't worry," he said with a conspiratorial wink, "your secret's safe. Maybe a little painting will make you feel better." He patted her shoulder and gave her a quick kiss on the cheek, then hurried down the stairs laughing to himself.

"I thought I'd feel better if I put on some makeup and washed my hair, that's all," Melissa called after him. She shook her head. So her father knew she was staying home to see Matt and Kirk. But he didn't seem to mind. *But what will Mom think?* wondered Melissa. She felt embarrassed suddenly. *Maybe I should tone the makeup down just a little,* she thought as she went back into the bathroom. She didn't want Matt and Kirk to think she was going out of her way to look good on their account. She toned down the eyeshadow and blush, but the lip gloss and mascara had to stay. They really did make her look better, maybe a little more sophisticated. Now she could get dressed.

Having decided not to go overboard trying to impress the guys, Melissa decided to wear her jeans and a white T-shirt instead of the white miniskirt she'd planned on. She glanced in the mirror and decided to add an over-sized pink vest to complete the outfit. After she strapped on her white sandals, she went to the mirror to see how she looked. The outfit definitely made the most of her slender figure. Her only complaint with the way she looked was that she would have liked to be about six inches taller, but there was nothing she could do about that.

While she was busy getting dressed, Melissa hadn't felt too anxious, but as she hurried down the steps to get some breakfast, she realized how nervous she was. This might be her one and only chance to make a real impression on

Matt and Kirk. If she blew it, she'd have to resign herself with saying hi to them when she ran into them at school. And then as mighty seniors they'd be too busy to pay attention to her or to get to know her.

"You look like you're feeling a little better this morning," Mrs. Darby said as Melissa came into the kitchen. Her mother was writing out some sort of list as she sipped her coffee. "I'm going to be out most of the day, so I thought you could take care of telling the boys what needs to be done." She looked at Melissa and smiled. "You wouldn't mind, would you?"

"No," Melissa said, trying not to blush. It was embarrassing to think her plan was so obvious to her parents. She hoped Matt and Kirk wouldn't see through her quite so easily. "I'm just going to spend the day reading, maybe watching a little TV. It won't be any trouble to help out."

"Well, you deserve a break," her mother said. She handed Melissa the list and gathered up her purse and the car keys. "There's plenty of food in the fridge if you want to offer them some lunch when they're finished. Have a good day."

Even if it was embarrassing, Melissa was pleased that her mom understood and was being so nice today.

Melissa was getting a bagel and wondering what to do so that it wouldn't seem as if she was just waiting around for Matt and Kirk to arrive, when the doorbell rang. She left her breakfast and went to answer it.

"Hey, the flower girl's home today," Matt kidded as Melissa opened the door. She smiled and stood back to let him in. Kirk was still at the car, busy untying the ladder. Melissa was admiring the way his hair gleamed in the sun when he pulled the ladder down, turned, and saw her.

"Hi!" he yelled, waving through the rungs of the ladder.

"Hi," Melissa called back, pushing her hair back from her face. She stood there holding the door open for Kirk and smiled. Her plan was going exactly the way she'd hoped!

Chapter Four

Melissa read off her mother's list of the things Matt and Kirk needed to do. They were supposed to start painting the downstairs rooms and Melissa offered to help move things and cover the furniture so they could get to the painting as soon as possible.

"So what happened to the flower shop?" Matt asked. "You didn't get fired because of what happened the other day, did you?" For a rare moment he was serious.

"Oh, no," Melissa assured him. "I just decided to take a day off to do nothing in particular. I might go to the beach this afternoon with some kids." Melissa didn't want it to be too obvious that she had stayed home just to see them. "So, what do you guys do when you're not painting?" she asked, hoping she sounded nonchalant.

"Matt spends most of his time driving other people crazy," Kirk said, rolling his eyes, "but *some* of us have responsibilities to live up to."

"Hey," Matt said indignantly. "I have to go to chemistry class this summer, don't forget about that."

Matt had managed to fail chemistry last term, Kirk explained, thanks to his penchant for practical jokes in the lab. "And if you pass this time it'll be a miracle. What did you do to Mrs. Ganz yesterday, anyway? I'll bet it was something horrible." Kirk smiled, obviously thinking about Matt's ongoing pranks on the chemistry teacher at Monroe, whom everybody loved to hate.

"Nothing major," Matt said with a grin. "I Krazy-glued her chalk to the desk. She practically went nuts trying to pick it up. Everyone was laughing, and finally she just stormed out of the room and came back with a new box of chalk. She tried to go on as if nothing had happened, but it was hard for the class to pay attention to the periodic table after all that."

"Aren't you afraid she'll fail you again?" Melissa asked incredulously.

"I bet she passes him just so she never has to see his face in her class again," Kirk said, laughing and shaking his head.

Matt grinned and nodded in agreement.

Melissa had heard all about Mrs. Ganz. She was supposed to be really tough, and everyone Melissa knew was afraid of her. It must have been a lot of fun to see her made to look so silly. Still, Melissa was amazed that Matt was so daring. It seemed like goofing around was the only thing Matt took seriously.

"So what do you do while Matt's harassing poor old Mrs. Ganz?" Melissa asked Kirk.

"Nothing nearly as exciting," Kirk said as he filled a roller tray with paint. "Lately I've been spending my afternoons watching my twin sisters. The babysitter quit two weeks ago and the new one doesn't start until September. So I'm stuck with two six-year-olds. Of course, it's not all that different from hanging around with Matt."

Matt lunged toward his friend with a wet paintbrush, just missing him. Kirk lunged back and suddenly the two were fencing with their brushes.

"Hey, watch out!" Melissa cried as they almost tipped over a bucket of paint. Kirk, the nimbler of the two, caught the bucket just in time, giving Matt the perfect opportunity to slather him with paint. Melissa laughed as Kirk tried to wipe the paint away with a rag. The whole left side of his face was now "antique sagebrush" green.

"You'll pay for that one," Kirk said menacingly. "But not now. We'd better not get too carried away. The Darbys probably wouldn't be too happy if they came home to find we'd painted their rug."

"What about their daughter?" Matt asked as he stepped toward Melissa, holding his brush up in front of him.

"No!" she shrieked, and jumped behind Kirk. "Save me. He's insane!" Before she knew what was happening, Kirk scooped her up in his arms and raced out of the room with her. She wrapped her arms tightly around his neck, afraid of falling. Melissa couldn't believe he was actually carrying her. She looked up into his shining, laughing brown eyes for a moment just before he dropped her unceremoniously onto the living room couch.

"Now, fair damsel," he said with a flourish, "you should be safe from the evil knight." Melissa laughed and looked up at him. "And I'd better get some work done. See you later."

After Kirk left the room, Melissa collapsed into the couch and smiled. She was so glad she'd stayed home from work today. She thought about how wonderful it had been to be in Kirk's arms, to stare into his eyes. And it was interesting to find out how the guys spent their afternoons.

There was just one thing that was beginning to bother Melissa a little. Unless she was over-reacting, she was beginning to think that Matt and Kirk liked her, maybe even a lot. But which one of them did she like better? Matt was the most easygoing, funniest person Melissa had ever met. She couldn't help laughing when he was around, and she couldn't imagine ever being bored around him. On the other hand, although Kirk had his silly moments, he also seemed to have a more serious side. And those eyes . . . Maybe Kirk was the cuter of the two. It was tough to decide.

Finally Melissa decided it didn't matter which one of the boys she liked better. After all, they were just friends, Melissa thought as she settled down to a historical romance.

Two hours later she headed for the room they were painting. "Aha!" Matt shouted as Melissa walked through the doorway. "She's back. Now I'll get her." He raised his brush and pointed it in her direction.

"Wait! Stop!" Melissa cried, holding up her hands in surrender. "I came to ask you if you want to stay for lunch. I felt so sorry for you when I read the note you left yesterday."

"Well, if you're going to feed us"—Matt lowered his brush and looked thoughtful—"I still might as well get you! Ha, ha!" Matt grabbed

Melissa before she had a chance to escape and very carefully dabbed her nose with paint. He held her tight around the waist and stared into her eyes for a minute, then let her go. "Now I've gotten you both," he said triumphantly.

Kirk and Melissa exchanged meaningful glances and slowly began to advance toward Matt.

"Of course, you realize," Melissa said, "that this means *war*!" She grabbed a paint roller and leapt at Matt. He was too close to the wall to get away, and Kirk pounced on him and held him while Melissa deftly swept the roller across his chest. "Revenge!" she cried. Kirk was about to take a stab at Matt with another wet brush when Matt suddenly looked toward the door and smiled innocently.

"Uh, hi, Mrs. Darby," Matt said, trying to act perfectly normal. Kirk let go of Matt and swung around to face the doorway.

Melissa was afraid to look. She hoped Matt was just trying to trick them.

"Melissa, what's going on?" That was definitely her mother's voice. Matt wasn't kidding around.

"Mom?" Melissa slowly turned around and tried to hide the incriminating paint roller behind her back. "You're home early." She knew she sounded silly.

Her mother just looked annoyed. "You boys

45

haven't gotten very much work done today, I see." It was true. They'd managed to paint only two walls in this room and there was no way they'd be able to start in the living room today. "You know this job is on a tight schedule as it is. I really don't think Mr. Darby will be very happy about this."

Matt and Kirk looked uncomfortable. Melissa realized that this was the first time she'd ever seen Matt at a loss for words.

"Sorry," Kirk said. "We'll get right back to work." He took the roller from Melissa, filled it with fresh paint, then climbed to the top of the ladder and started to paint. Mrs. Darby glared at Melissa, then turned and left the room.

"I guess we won't have time for lunch, after all," Matt said lightheartedly. "But I'll take a rain check."

Melissa smiled weakly. "I'd better go," she said. "I don't want you guys to lose your job because of all of this."

Melissa left the room to go face her mother. She found her in the kitchen.

"I'm sorry, Mom," Melissa said, contrite. "I don't know how things got so out of hand, but they've really been working almost the whole time since they got here. I just went in to invite them to lunch and—"

"Melissa, you have green paint on your nose,"

Mrs. Darby said. Melissa could tell she was still angry, but there was an amused twinkle in her eyes. Melissa quickly reached up and felt her nose, then grabbed a paper towel and wiped at it. The paint had dried already.

"I think you'll have to use turpentine," her mother said with a laugh.

For some reason Melissa found her mother's laughter more upsetting than her anger. "Oh, Mother," she cried, and ran upstairs to her room.

A few minutes later Mrs. Darby knocked on her door. "Can I come in?" she asked.

"Sure," Melissa said grudgingly. The door opened and her mother came into the room. She was carrying a rag that smelled of paint thinner.

"I thought you might need this," she said, handing the rag to Melissa. "Just try not to breathe the fumes while you're cleaning the paint off."

Melissa took the rag and went to stand in front of her mirror. When she saw herself she couldn't help laughing a little.

"I'm sorry I laughed at you, but it really does look funny," Mrs. Darby said. She came closer and hugged Melissa's shoulders. "I know you're interested in Kirk and Matt, and it must be fun for you to have them here and paying you a lot of attention, but they do have to get their work done."

"I know, Mom," Melissa began, "but—"

"Wait," continued her mother. "I'm happy you're all getting along so well, and I'm glad you're not moping around missing Jill and Amy so much. Just try not to let things get out of control again, okay?"

"Okay," Melissa agreed. She made a face at herself in the mirror. She'd gotten most of the paint off her nose, but she still looked a little weird.

Melissa made sandwiches and when Matt and Kirk were finished working, they sat outside and had an impromptu picnic. Matt seemed subdued and the three of them talked not about Matt's wild antics but about school, people they knew in common, even soccer. By the time the guys left, Melissa wasn't so worried about not seeing them again. Somehow their painting escapade earlier in the day had cemented their new friendship.

"So will you be home tomorrow?" Kirk asked as Melissa helped him carry the ladder to the car.

"No, I'll be at the flower shop all day tomorrow," Melissa answered, pleased that he'd asked.

"Maybe I'll stop by and say hello," Kirk said.

"Just don't bring Matt along," Melissa joked. "I don't want to lose my job!"

Just then Matt joined them with the buckets and brushes. "Don't bring Matt along where?" he asked, pretending to be hurt.

"Anywhere," Melissa said, giving him a playful shove. "You've gotten me in too much trouble already. You'd better not come by to see me at work again unless you can control yourself." She laughed and Matt smiled at her.

"All right, I promise not to visit you at work," Matt said. "If I need to buy more flowers, I'll go to Simpson's instead." Simpson's was the other local flower shop, Mr. Grover's competition.

"You'd better not!" Melissa chided him.

"Come on," Kirk called to Matt, "I've got to get home. The little monsters will be waiting."

Matt hopped into the car and started it up.

"Bye," Melissa called, waving. They honked and waved, then drove away. Melissa felt happy as she turned back toward the house. All in all, it had been a great day.

Melissa was actually looking forward to work when she got up the next morning. Maybe Kirk or Matt would even come by to visit. She took special care with her makeup and wore her favorite white jeans. She even decided not to braid her hair, but caught it up in a high ponytail.

Mr. Grover seemed relieved to see her when she arrived at the shop.

"I'm glad you're feeling better," he said. "Yesterday was quiet, but today we'll be very busy. We've got orders for dozens of corsages thanks to the big country club anniversary party tonight."

"Well, let's get started then," Melissa said cheerfully.

The first thing to do was unload the boxes of delicate orchids that had arrived. Once they were safely stored, she and Mr. Grover got to work. The orchids and tea roses were beautiful but also especially delicate, so it took careful handling to keep them in good condition. As each corsage was made, it went into a small plastic box filled with a nest of cellophane grass. As the day progressed, the refrigerator became filled with boxes. Since she had stayed home the day before, Melissa offered to work through the afternoon to help get all the corsages made.

Mr. Grover had just gone out to get them some lunch from the deli down the street when the bell over the door jingled. Melissa looked up to see Kirk coming into the shop. Behind him were two little girls with shiny blond pigtails.

"Hi," Melissa said as they came toward the counter. "These must be your sisters." She slipped off her stool and went around to meet them.

"This is Lynn," Kirk said, pointing to the girl

50

wearing pink shorts and a T-shirt, "and this is Sandy." Sandy was wearing an identical outfit except that hers was yellow. Melissa wouldn't have been able to tell the girls apart if they hadn't been dressed differently. "I'm taking them to the park and I just thought we'd stop by on our way."

Melissa noticed that Kirk seemed different, quieter, almost shy today. Maybe it was because his sisters were with him.

"Would you girls like a flower?" she asked when she noticed them eyeing the refrigerator full of blossoms.

"Yes! Oh, yes," the girls cried together. Melissa took them to a section where there were pretty flowers that weren't too exotic. Mr. Grover wouldn't mind if she gave away a couple of daisies or snapdragons, but the orchids and roses were a different matter.

While the girls were busy looking through the glass at the flowers, trying to decide what they wanted, Kirk turned to Melissa.

"I was wondering," Kirk finally said, "are you busy Saturday afternoon?"

Melissa felt a rush of excitement. Kirk was asking her out on a date! She hadn't expected that.

"No, I'm just going to be home, doing stuff around the house." She waited expectantly for him to go on.

"Great," he said, "would you like to go sailing? My parents are taking the girls to the zoo, so I'll have the afternoon to myself. We could have a picnic."

"That sounds fantastic," Melissa said. "I'm not much of a sailor, but I'd love to learn. And I'm a good swimmer, if that helps." She couldn't think of a better way to spend Saturday than sailing around the lake with Kirk Gardener. *Wow*, she thought, *Amy and Jill will never believe this!*

"I'd like one of those red ones," Lynn said to Melissa, tugging her arm and pointing to the carnations.

"And I want one of those," Sandy said, pointing to a big bright daisy.

Melissa got the girls their flowers and on impulse pulled out a white carnation to give to Kirk.

"I'll treasure it always," he said, smiling as he poked it through a buttonhole on his shirt. As he was herding the girls out the door, he turned and said, "I'll pick you up around noon, all right?"

"That sounds great," Melissa said, and smiled. The girls waved goodbye with their flowers and scurried past Kirk toward the car.

As they were leaving, Mr. Grover returned with lunch.

"I hope you don't mind," Melissa said to her boss as he unpacked their sandwiches, "but my friend dropped by to say hi and I gave his little sisters each a flower. They got such a kick out of picking them out."

Mr. Grover smiled. "I'd much rather you give a couple of flowers to two little girls than see you tangoing in the store."

Melissa blushed, remembering that embarrassing episode. "Good chicken salad," she said, munching her sandwich and hoping to change the subject.

The rest of the day went by quietly. Melissa was happy daydreaming about Saturday and her date with Kirk as she put together one corsage after another. It wasn't until late in the day, when she was almost finished with her work, that she wondered if Kirk had taken her seriously when she'd said not to bring Matt by the store. Or maybe he didn't want Matt to know he was asking her out. Well, she could ask him when she saw him on Saturday. She probably wouldn't see Matt before then anyway, and there wasn't any reason for her to mention to Matt that she and Kirk had a date. Was there?

Chapter Five

When she got home from work, Melissa felt as if she was going to burst if she didn't tell someone the news about her date with Kirk. If only Amy were home, or Jill. Since they weren't, Mrs. Darby was the first one to hear Melissa's news.

"Mom, I have a date on Saturday," Melissa said, trying not to sound as wildly excited as she was. "I can go, can't I?"

"Well, that depends on who the date is with and what you're planning to do, I suppose," Mrs. Darby said.

"Kirk asked me out," Melissa said. "He came by the flower shop today. He wants to take me sailing on Saturday!"

54

"That sounds wonderful, sweetheart," Mrs. Darby said. "Kirk seems like a responsible boy, and he's awfully cute, too. But is he an experienced sailor? Will you two be out on the water alone?"

"He's a terrific sailor, Mom. It will just be the two of us, but he sails all the time. His family has a boat. He wouldn't have asked me if it wasn't safe." Melissa was suddenly worried that her mother would have one of her overprotectiveness attacks and say no to the sailing.

"Well, would you mind if I called his parents just to ease my mind about this?"

Melissa weighed her embarrassment at having her mother call Kirk's family against her fear that if her mom didn't call she wouldn't have a chance to go sailing at all.

"All right," Melissa grumbled. "But please, don't make too big a deal about it, okay?"

"I promise," her mother said earnestly. She went to the phone and dialed Kirk's number. From what Melissa could hear, the conversation was short and sweet. She could tell after a minute that her mother was impressed with whatever Kirk's mother had to say about his sailing ability.

"It looks like you'll be sailing on Saturday," Mrs. Darby said after she hung up.

"Oh, thanks, Mom!" Melissa gave her mother a big hug, then hurried up to her room. She wanted to write to Amy and Jill about *this* right away.

The next day at work Melissa was floating on air. The more she thought about Kirk, the more she realized she liked him. And going sailing alone together on a quiet, peaceful lake was a perfect way to get to know him even better.

Melissa spent a good part of the day planning what to wear and finally decided she'd have to go shopping for a new bathing suit right after work. Closing her eyes, she imagined Kirk kissing her. How would it feel? she wondered. Would they melt into each other's arms effortlessly? Or would it be sort of hesitant and awkward? She couldn't imagine Kirk being hesitant over anything, but maybe kissing was different. Maybe even guys as popular as Kirk got nervous about it. Either way, she hoped he wasn't a sloppy kisser. That was *too* disgusting! No, she decided, if and when Kirk Gardener ever kissed her, it would be perfect.

Melissa sighed. It was a good thing the shop wasn't very busy. In fact, if she hadn't been so preoccupied thinking about Kirk, Melissa would probably have been bored out of her mind. Mr. Grover had been out of the shop most of the morning making deliveries and she'd had only two small arrangements to do. Even the phone had been quiet.

Melissa was just packing up to go home when the bell jingled. "Rats," she whispered. She really wanted to leave as soon as Mr. Grover got back so that she could go shopping for that new bathing suit. Now she'd have to stay and deal with a customer. But when she turned around, Melissa jumped back in surprise; Matt was leaning against the counter, a devilish grin on his face and a rose between his teeth.

"Oh, no," Melissa squealed, "not again." She grabbed the rose away from him and stuck it into a vase. "Have you come to buy flowers to make up for playing another terrible trick on your poor mother?" she asked, raising an eyebrow.

"No," Matt said, looking wounded. "Whatever gave you an idea like that? Actually, I stopped by to see if you're busy tonight."

Melissa could only stare at him in surprise. Matt was asking her out . . . on a *date*? In her wildest dreams she'd never expected that! She was totally taken aback.

"Um, well . . ." She hesitated, thinking that maybe she should mention something about going out with Kirk. "Well, I have to go shopping this afternoon. But I'm free after that. Why?"

"Some kids are going to the lake on the Highland estate tonight and then out for dinner at Pete's. I thought you'd like to come along. It should be a real blast. The moon will be full, so it'll be a great night for a swim." He flashed her his most charming smile, his bright blue eyes twinkling under his shaggy bangs.

Melissa really couldn't resist. It sounded too romantic—swimming in the moonlight. And there wasn't really any reason to mention her date with Kirk. Unless . . .

"Will Kirk be there, too?" Melissa asked casually.

"No, he's not really into that sort of thing. Besides, he and I aren't Siamese twins, you know. We don't do *everything* together." Matt winked at her.

"Well, it sounds like a lot of fun," Melissa said, smiling. "I'll just have to make sure it's all right with my parents."

"I'll call you around seven and you can let me know then," offered Matt. "Gotta get to chemistry class. Bye." Matt grinned at Melissa as he turned to leave the shop. When he got to the door, he looked at her again. He had another rose between his teeth.

"You owe me three dollars for that," she called, trying not to laugh. Matt just waved to her and slipped out the door.

As soon as Mr. Grover got back, Melissa got her things together, said goodbye to him, and headed for her car. She was anxious to get home and tell her parents she was going out tonight, but she had to go shopping first. Suddenly she wasn't sure what to be more excited about. Sailing with Kirk would be wonderful and romantic, but going out with Matt and a bunch of other seniors would be really exciting. And it sounded so daring. The lake at the Highland estate was private property, and going swimming there was a pretty wild thing to do. This was her chance to be part of the cool gang.

Miraculously, Melissa found the perfect bathing suit at the first store she went to. It was a one-piece, cut high at the thighs with a plunging back and halter top. It was sparkly white and it looked great on her. She decided to splurge and buy a new pair of sandals, pretty white ones with skinny straps and tiny turquoise beads, and a bright turquoise sundress with a full skirt and spaghetti straps. All she needed now was some new makeup. She picked out a shimmering blue eyeliner that matched her dress and a tube of pearly pink lip gloss. Now she was set for both dates.

"Hi, Mom," Melissa called as she came through the front door.

"I'm upstairs," her mother called back.

Melissa ran up the stairs, threw her shopping bags into her room, and went in to see her mother.

"Matt invited me to have dinner with him and some other kids tonight, okay?" Melissa told her mom, trying to make the evening sound as innocent as possible. She didn't think her mother would approve of her swimming at the Highland estate, so she decided not to mention that part of her plans.

"You certainly are popular," Mrs. Darby replied with a smile. "Sure, that sounds all right. What time are you leaving?"

"Mmm, I'm not sure," Melissa answered. "Matt's going to call later to let me know."

"Is Kirk going along, too?" her mother asked.

Melissa wasn't sure what to say. Would it make any difference to her mother?

"I don't think so," Melissa said, not wanting to lie. "I think he's busy doing something else." Melissa went to her room, anxious to try on her new outfits and play around with her new makeup. She'd planned to wear an old bathing suit to swim in tonight, but then it occurred to her that her new shimmery suit would look great in the moonlight. She tried it on again and primped in front of the mirror.

Melissa was startled by a knock on her door. It was her mother.

"Wow," Mrs. Darby said. "That's a pretty glamorous bathing suit. Is it for tomorrow?"

Melissa smiled. She was about to say that

60

she'd decided to wear it tonight because of the moonlight but caught herself. She twirled around. "What do you think?"

"Do you think Kirk will like it?" Melissa asked, spinning around to give her mother a better view. She held out her foot to display her new sandals.

"You look terrific," Mrs. Darby said. "I just wanted to let you know I'm leaving to meet Dad downtown. We'll see you later, by eleven, right?"

"Right," Melissa agreed. She didn't think she'd have any trouble being home by her curfew tonight. "Bye."

The phone rang at a little past seven, and Matt said he'd be right over. Quickly, Melissa dashed upstairs to give her makeup a final check and grab her purse. When the doorbell rang a few minutes later, Melissa flew down the stairs and opened the door. Her breath caught in her throat when she saw Matt. He had on a pink-and-white-striped Oxford shirt and jeans—and he looked completely gorgeous. Running a hand through his longish brown hair, he said, "You look terrific. Ready to go?"

"Just let me get my towel," she said, dashing inside for a beach towel. "Let's go," she said cheerfully.

Melissa wasn't surprised to discover that Matt was a crazy driver. In fact, she realized the only thing about Matt that might surprise her at this point was if he did something that was *normal.*

"We can park just off the main road by the back gate to the estate," Matt explained. "Everybody's supposed to be meeting there at eight."

"How do we get in?" wondered Melissa, feeling brash and wild herself.

"Oh, Jim Canon figured out how to spring the padlock, so we'll just open the gate and walk right through. It's about a mile walk through the woods to the lake. You've never been there before, huh?" Matt glanced at her and grinned. "You'll love it. It's really pretty."

"What about the guards?" Melissa asked. "I've heard they patrol the grounds with attack dogs." That was one thing she was a little worried about, but she didn't want to seem like a goody-goody.

"Oh, don't worry." Matt laughed, reaching over to give her shoulder a reassuring squeeze. "I'll protect you. Besides, I've been coming here all summer and we haven't seen any guards. Relax, it'll be fun. Promise."

When they got to the gate Matt had described, Melissa saw three other couples waiting. A guy she recognized as Jim Canon was leaning against the gate, obviously working on the lock. She didn't know the other two boys, but the girls seemed vaguely familiar. She'd seen them at soccer games and realized that one of them was Susan Thatcher, a cheerleader. Melissa felt a little awkward suddenly. These kids had a reputation for being rowdy and pretty wild. She wasn't sure if she'd fit in. Still, she was with Matt, so they'd have to accept her for tonight at least.

"This is Melissa," Matt said, introducing her to the group. Everyone said hi and then ignored her. All eyes were focused on Jim and the lock.

"Ha! Got it," he said as the lock sprang open. "Ladies first." He gallantly bowed and the girls hurried through the gate, followed by the boys. As soon as they got into the woods, it got very dark. There was a narrow trail that was sometimes overgrown with brush, and Melissa had a hard time making her way along in her fancy sandals. She noticed everyone else had worn sneakers.

Melissa was stumbling over a particularly prickly bush when suddenly she heard a bark behind her. She jumped back toward Matt and grabbed his arm.

"Listen," she said nervously. "The attack dogs!" She was really frightened. Then she heard it again, but it was too close, right by her ear. . . .

"Grrr," Matt growled, and barked again be-

63

fore he broke down into a fit of hysterical laughter. Everyone else was laughing, too—except Melissa. She let go of Matt's arm and started down the path again, not looking back.

"Very funny," she called as she shoved her way through the woods. Matt caught up with her easily. He was still laughing.

"Sorry," he said. "I was just teasing. I didn't mean to scare you." He put his arm around Melissa's shoulder and pulled her toward him. "Really." He hugged her and smiled. "I'm sorry."

She looked up into his eyes and saw genuine concern mixed in with the laughter. He still thought it was funny, but he was obviously sorry, too.

"Let's just get to the lake," Melissa grumbled, cracking a small smile. She didn't like being the brunt of Matt's joke and she was kind of embarrassed that she'd been the only one who'd fallen for Matt's trick. On the other hand, being hugged hadn't been all bad. And she had to admit, if the joke had been on somebody else, she would have laughed, too.

After what seemed like hours there was finally a clearing visible ahead. Moonlight lit the last few yards of the trail and made it much easier going.

"Oh, it's beautiful," Melissa gasped as she came out of the woods and got her first glimpse of the lake. They were up on a rocky ledge that jutted out over the water. Reflections of the full moon and glittering stars shimmered on its dark surface, and the sky was a deep violet. The lake was surrounded by dark patches of trees and rocky ledges like the one they stood on. Melissa would have been happy to just sit and look, but everyone quickly began stripping down to their bathing suits. After all, she thought, they'd been coming here all summer; the view probably wasn't nearly as spectacular to them anymore.

"Come on, let's go swimming," Matt said, impatiently pulling her braid. Melissa carefully pulled the top of her bathing suit up under her sundress, then slipped out of the dress and her sandals. It was such a romantic place that Melissa suddenly almost wished she and Matt could be alone. It would be kind of nice just to sit and talk.

"Geronimo!" Matt shouted as he raced to the end of the rock and leapt into the water, making a tremendous splash.

"Hey!" Melissa cried out, suddenly dripping wet. "You did that on purpose!"

Matt looked up guiltily and she had to smile. "Here goes nothing," she shouted, and took a running dive into the water.

"I was afraid you'd turn out to be one of those

girls who's afraid to get her hair wet," Matt teased, swimming over to Melissa. The water was wonderfully warm.

"This really is beautiful, Matt," Melissa said, treading water. "I'm glad you invited me."

"Me too." He looked at her seriously, and Melissa felt a warm tingle shoot through her. He looked like he was about to say something else when someone swam over to them.

"Come on, you guys, we're going to play water tag," the boy said.

"Great idea!" Matt shouted. "I'll be 'it.'"

Soon everyone was shrieking and laughing as they tried to get away from him. Melissa was sorry they'd been interrupted just when Matt seemed about to tell her something important, but soon she was swept up in the fun.

"Good thing you're wearing a one-piece," a girl named Beth said to Melissa as they raced away from Matt. "Otherwise you'd have to worry about him trying to untie your bikini top." Suddenly Matt lunged at them. Beth, who was wearing a bikini, screamed and dived underwater, escaping by a hair, but Melissa wasn't quick enough. Not that she minded being tagged. Matt grabbed her and pulled her toward him.

"Got you!" he shouted, and unexpectedly gave her a quick kiss on the cheek. Then he disappeared. Melissa was so stunned, it took her a minute to realize that she now had to chase the rest of the group. She was about to dive underwater and swim toward Jim, who was closest to her.

"Hey, what was that?" Matt whispered urgently. Everyone stopped to listen.

"Just another one of your jokes, I bet." Melissa laughed. Then she heard it, too . . . the sound of dogs barking. Around a bend in the lake not too far from the trail they'd come down, Melissa saw the beams of three flashlights.

Chapter Six

"Jeez," Jim said, "let's get out of here." Everyone swam to the edge of the lake and began climbing out of the water. The rock ledge that had been so perfect for diving off was now a problem. It was a slow climb to get back up to where they had left their clothes, and by the time they'd gotten half-dressed, the guards were close enough to see them in the moonlight.

"Hey, you kids!" one of them yelled. The dogs barked ferociously and strained at their leashes. Melissa fumbled with her sandals, unable to get the straps buckled because she was so nervous.

"Come on!" Matt whispered, pulling her up and dragging her toward the path. Somehow Melissa managed to finish buckling her shoe, hopping as she hurried along with the others. At first she was scared, but as the group got farther ahead of the guards and their barking dogs, Melissa began to enjoy the thrill of getting away. By the time they reached the gate, everyone was laughing. They paused for a moment to catch their breath and gloat over their escape, but when the barking began to sound close again, they ran to their cars.

"See you at Pete's," Matt called to the others as he and Melissa raced away. "Well, I guess I owe you an apology," Matt said after they'd been driving awhile.

"What for?" Melissa asked. She felt totally exhilarated. This was definitely the most exciting thing she'd ever done. Jill and Amy would be very impressed.

"You were right about those dogs," he said, laughing again. "I almost feel guilty for scaring you earlier. Almost."

"Don't think I've forgotten about that," Melissa quipped. "Someday, when you least expect it, I will have my revenge. Don't forget the paint roller." They both laughed, remembering the day of the paint fight with Kirk. Matt certainly got her into a lot of close calls, Melissa thought. But even so, she'd never had so much fun with anyone.

*　　*　　*

"I hope you're hungry," Matt said as they pulled into the parking lot at Pete's.

"Starving," Melissa answered. Swimming and running through the woods had given her a tremendous appetite. She couldn't wait to sink her teeth into a delicious hamburger. She was also looking forward to walking into Pete's with Matt and sitting with the rest of the group. Everyone hung out at Pete's. Melissa and Jill and Amy had their special booth where they usually sat and gossiped, watching enviously as the more popular kids flitted around the place. Together they planned strategies for improving their popularity, meeting boys they liked, and making themselves over. Now, tonight, Melissa actually *was* one of the popular kids, sort of.

As she passed the booth where she usually sat, Melissa felt proud of herself. She wouldn't have to just sit on the sidelines and watch anymore. Now everyone would know she was part of the in-crowd. It was hard to believe that two weeks ago she and Amy and Jill had lamented their lack of boyfriends and worried about their social lives. Melissa looked at Matt, admiring his amazing smile and his twinkling blue eyes. It was incredible to think that this tall, gorgeous guy had actually kissed her—if you counted kisses on the cheek, which Melissa did—and held her in his arms. Remembering those moments with Matt made Melissa tingle. She still couldn't believe that he was interested in her.

"Do you ever come here?" Matt asked her as they sat down with the rest of the group. Melissa felt a little chagrined to think of how many times she'd sat in her booth and gawked at Matt and yet he'd never even known she existed.

"Once in a while," she said. There was no point in calling attention to her spectacular unnoticeability. "It's a great place."

"Oh, I've seen you here before," Susan piped up. She was sitting on the other side of Matt, with her chair extra close to his. She leaned across Matt toward Melissa as she spoke. "You usually sit over in the corner there, don't you? With that girl who's on the tennis team—what's her name?" Susan smiled cattily and Melissa wanted to strangle her. Suddenly she realized that Susan either had, or wanted to have, some sort of claim on Matt.

"You must mean Jill Ansel," Melissa said calmly, hoping to avoid a scene.

Luckily, the waitress arrived at that moment and everyone who had heard Susan's pointed comments got involved in ordering food. Matt seemed completely oblivious to the tension.

"I'll have a double bacon cheeseburger, medium rare, with french fries, onion rings, and a chocolate shake," Matt said. The waitress had trouble writing as fast as he ordered and she'd just finished when Matt said, "On second thought, make that a Pete's Special with no onion, extra mushrooms, an order of fried zucchini, and . . ." Matt paused and stared at the menu, seemingly incapable of deciding what he wanted. It was late Friday night and the restaurant was packed with people.

"Why don't you take my order," Melissa offered, trying to help out the busy waitress while Matt figured out what he wanted to eat.

"Wait a minute," Matt said, flashing the waitress his most dazzling smile. "I'm really sorry to be such a bother. Maybe you could help me decide. Which is better, a double bacon cheeseburger or a Pete's Special?"

"Oh, brother, is that ever a corny line," groaned Susan.

But the waitress didn't seem to mind. She actually smiled at Matt. "I'd say the double bacon cheeseburger is better."

"Then that's what I'll have," Matt said, handing her his menu.

Melissa was amazed at how easily Matt had charmed the waitress. If he'd asked her to, she would have waited all night for him to order.

While they waited for their food to come, everyone talked about their great escape from the guards at Highland lake. Other kids stopped by the table to hear about it, and with each telling, the story got wilder and the dogs got more and more vicious. Melissa was pleased to think that soon this story would be circulating all over school—everyone would know that she had been one of the incredibly daring kids who were there. They'd also know that she'd been Matt Warner's date for the evening. Melissa felt sure that she had moved up into the sphere of real popularity.

The food took a long time to arrive and Melissa had plenty of time to talk with Matt and his friends. She thought she'd finally have a chance to get to know a little more about Matt, but somehow the conversation always revolved around some crazy thing he had just done or was planning to do. He was entertaining everyone with tales of the tricks he'd played in chemistry class this week. And though Melissa enjoyed the stories and laughed as hard as anyone else, she felt a little disappointed that she and Matt weren't going to have any time alone. He didn't seem to have any interest in really talking to her or learning more about her. Matt occasionally glanced at her and smiled, but it wasn't nearly as often as she would have liked. As for the rest of the crowd, they seemed completely indifferent to her being there, except of course for Susan, who periodically glared at Melissa for no reason at all.

As Matt launched into yet another story about his pranks, Melissa realized she was getting bored. It seemed impossible. After all, here she was with the guy of her dreams and the super-popular crowd.

When Melissa tuned back into the conversation, everyone was laughing as Jim poured his leftover shake onto his plate and mashed it into his fries.

"Talk about weirdos, what are you doing?" Susan asked. "That's the most revolting mess I've ever seen."

Melissa found herself silently agreeing.

"Your plate's no door prize, either," Matt teased, looking down at her shredded bits of half-eaten sandwich.

Pretty soon everyone was trying to outgross everyone else. By the time they finished, there were three ketchup-and-chocolate shakes and piles of mashed-up food on everyone's plate. Jim's was by far the worst. After he'd squished the fries and shake together, he'd poured pepper all over it, then a little salt, and finally half a glass of Coke. When the soggy fries were floating in an ice-cream and soda lake, he added Susan's pickles to top it off.

Melissa felt a little guilty about the mess they'd made. She sure didn't envy whoever had to clean it up. And what would the waitress think of them? They'd probably never be allowed to come back. And talk about immature, Melissa thought. My brother does that—but he's only nine! She was glad when everyone decided it was time to leave.

Melissa was hoping that she'd never have that waitress again as the group wandered out into the parking lot, the conversation still loud and boisterous and back on the subject of the great escape from the guards and dogs at Highland lake.

"Oh, no," Susan squealed suddenly. "It's midnight! My parents are going to kill me if I'm late again."

Midnight? How could it be midnight? Melissa thought. "Matt, I was supposed to be home by eleven," she said, stunned. She'd totally lost track of the time. Her parents were probably ready to call out the police to find her. "I've got to get home right away."

"Don't worry," Matt said with a laugh. "I'll come up with a story that'll keep your parents from grounding you for life." They got in the car.

"What can you say to them?" Melissa asked Matt as they sped along the road. "What explanation can there be for being so late and not even calling? I'm doomed." Melissa slumped down in her seat. What would she tell Kirk if she were grounded and couldn't go out with him tomorrow? Then Melissa noticed her dress. In all the excitement she hadn't realized that she'd ripped it along the hem, probably when she was running through the woods. But that wasn't the worst of it. There were nettles and dirt all over it, as well. How could she explain that? She was a total wreck. "Oh, no," she groaned, imagining her parents' faces when she walked in the house.

"Relax," Matt said, reaching over to pat her on the leg. "I have a plan."

As they pulled into the driveway, the front porch door opened and Melissa's parents stepped outside. Melissa brushed off her skirt and tried to smooth over the ripped place in her dress. She didn't want to get out of the car, but Matt opened his door and greeted her parents as if nothing was wrong. She had no choice but to follow him.

"I'm so sorry to keep Melissa out so late," Matt began before either of her parents had a chance to ask what was going on. "I was held up at another painting job and couldn't get here till almost nine. Poor Melissa had given up on me and when we got to Pete's nobody else was there. I thought we had plenty of time to stop by Jim Canon's on the way home, but I didn't count on having car trouble." Matt finally paused. Mr. and Mrs. Darby were hooked now, and they waited expectantly for him to finish his explanation.

Mrs. Darby glanced at Melissa, who had come to stand on the porch next to Matt. "Melissa, your dress!" she said, her eyes wide. "What on earth happened to you?"

"Mom, I—" Melissa began.

"It's my fault," Matt interrupted. "My transmission jammed and we had to get out of the car on the side of the road. Unfortunately, Melissa had to wade through a bunch of weeds."

"It was a real mess," said Melissa, amazed that her parents were buying Matt's ridiculous story.

"I'll be happy to pay for the dress," Matt added. "I'm just glad I was able to get the car into gear again to get us back here safely."

"Do you think it's safe for you to drive the car home?" Mrs. Darby asked.

"I'd be happy to take you home," Mr. Darby added. "You can have someone come look at the car tomorrow."

"That's okay," Matt said. "I'm a pretty good mechanic, so I'll be able to fix it at home. As long as I don't have to shift too much, I should get there just fine." Matt smiled one of his beautiful, dazzling smiles. "So, I guess I'll just say good night. Sorry about all this, Melissa. Maybe next time we can take your car." He laughed and patted her on the back, then winked and turned to go, smiling like a Cheshire cat. Melissa was speechless.

"Come on in," her father said, putting an

arm around her and pulling her toward the door.

"Are you hungry, dear?" Mrs. Darby asked. "Did you manage to get any dinner? What will we do with that dress?"

"Thanks, Mom," Melissa said, "but I think I'll just go to bed. I don't have much of an appetite right now."

As they climbed the stairs and headed for bed, Melissa felt vaguely guilty. She'd expected to be grounded and lectured and here was her mother offering to fix her a midnight supper. Matt seemed to have magical powers over people. It wasn't until she had slid into bed and replayed the night's events in her head that Melissa realized she hadn't even gotten a kiss good night from Matt. In all the confusion she hadn't even had a chance to be nervous about it.

He had kissed her when they were swimming, but that had seemed so playful. And what about Susan? Where did she fit in? Melissa lay in bed unable to fall asleep, trying to figure out just what sort of a date she'd had with Matt.

In fact, Melissa realized that she still didn't know much of anything about Matt—except, of course, that he was completely crazy.

Melissa snuggled down into her pillow. Jill and Amy would laugh till they cried when she told them about this date. She really had had a good time. Melissa would never forget how beautiful the lake had looked glittering under the full moon. Of course, being chased by wild guard dogs had been pretty exciting, too.

Finally, Melissa drifted off to sleep. All night long she dreamed of barking dogs chasing giant hamburgers through the woods to the sound of Matt's infectious laughter.

Chapter Seven

A sharp knock on her bedroom door woke Melissa the next morning. "Melissa," her mother said as she opened the door. "Aren't you supposed to be going out today?"

Melissa rubbed her eyes and groggily reached for her clock. It was eleven-thirty.

"Oh, no!" she cried, leaping out of bed. "Kirk will be here in half an hour."

"Shall I fix you something to eat?" Mrs. Darby called as Melissa raced to the bathroom and turned on the shower.

"No, thanks." She jumped under the still-cold water. Why hadn't she stayed up and washed her hair last night? Melissa wanted to impress Kirk today and had planned to wear her hair loose. But even though she'd kept it braided, it was a mess after swimming in the lake. She frantically scrubbed shampoo and then conditioner through her long locks. "Come on," she whispered impatiently as she rinsed and rinsed. It seemed to take hours to get the conditioner out. She'd have to wear her hair braided after all. There was no time to dry it.

As she smoothed suntan lotion over her arms, Melissa noticed her bathing suit slung over a chair along with her ruined dress.

"No!" she gasped, picking up the suit. An ugly snag wound all the way around the front. The suit was ruined, too. She must have caught it on something in her rush up the rocky ledge in the dark last night. Now she'd have to wear one of her old suits. Disgusted, Melissa tossed the shimmering white bathing suit into her trash can and began rummaging through her drawers to find another one. She'd have to choose between the striped maillot that looked like a reject from the swim team and the red bikini that she'd bought on a dare from Amy and never actually wore in public.

Downstairs, the doorbell rang and Melissa heard her father greet Kirk. She slipped into the bikini and took a quick look in the mirror. It was very daring, but it looked great. She pulled a sweatshirt and shorts over the suit and grabbed her sandals and purse.

Makeup, she thought. The shimmery pink lipstick and blue eyeshadow she'd bought yesterday really wouldn't work with a red-hot bikini. Searching through her makeup, she found a clear red lip gloss and a waterproof gray eyeliner. She had enough of a tan that she could skip the blush.

"Melissa," her father called. "Kirk's here." Melissa ran to the bathroom and carefully applied a thin line of gray around her eyes.

"Be right down," she hollered as she smudged the liner. She put on the lip gloss and looked at herself critically. She was surprised at how together she looked. The gray liner really accented her hazel eyes. Suddenly she felt glamorous and exotic. Maybe Kirk would be impressed even though her hair was in a stupid braid.

Feeling full of confidence and a little out of breath, Melissa headed for the stairs, then raced back to her room when she remembered she'd forgotten earrings. The pair she picked out were the perfect finishing touch: big gold hoops.

"Hi," Kirk said as Melissa finally appeared. "You look great." Melissa smiled. She noticed her mother raise an eyebrow. Melissa did look a little more sophisticated than usual. Thank goodness her mother hadn't seen the bikini!

"Sorry to keep you waiting," she said to Kirk. "Guess we'd better get going." She turned to say goodbye to her parents. "And don't worry, I promise to wear my life jacket," she teased them.

"Just don't be home too late this time," Mr. Darby said.

Melissa was suddenly afraid her father would spill the beans about last night. "I'll call later and let you know when to expect me home," she said, pushing the door open. She was anxious to get out of the house before it was too late.

"So long," Kirk said amiably.

Melissa breathed a sigh of relief as she settled into the front seat of Kirk's car.

"Have you been breaking your curfew?" Kirk asked playfully as they drove away.

"Oh, you mean because of what my father said?" Melissa tried to sound casual. "That was no big deal. So, tell me about sailing," she said quickly, changing the subject.

"It's hard to know where to begin. I've been around boats ever since I was a few months old. My mom and dad are really into sailing, and they taught us kids how to handle ourselves around boats as soon as we were old enough to walk, just about."

"So you must have spent every summer out on the lake when you were growing up," Melissa said.

"Sure," Kirk answered. "There was this huge group of kids all around the same age who hung out together. We all learned to sail about the same time, and we'd have these races in the summer. We never took it all that seriously, though. I mean, we liked to win and all, but it was always more fun than anything else.

"I remember one race a couple of years ago," he went on. "It was in late August, and it was cloudy and pretty cold outside. The boat we had then was pretty fast, but the pin that held the rudder on was broken and we had to keep jumping overboard and fixing it as we went. Doug Martin—this guy I grew up with—and I were so cold and wet by the time we finished the race, we swore we'd never go out again."

"But you did, didn't you," Melissa prompted.

Kirk looked at her briefly, then turned back toward the road. "Yeah," he admitted with a laugh. "We went sailing the next day. And you know, even though we were miserable during that race, it's one of my best memories from that summer. We even finished second."

"Wow, even though your . . . rudder?"—Kirk nodded—"your rudder was broken? That's great!" Melissa suddenly wanted to know more. "Do you still race?"

"Sometimes," Kirk said. Then he shrugged. "Most of the kids I sailed with back then have summer jobs, and girlfriends or boyfriends to keep them busy. But once in a while, we still get together."

"It sounds like sailing really means a lot to you."

"I don't know what I'll do if I don't get into a college where I can sail," Kirk replied. "I'm applying to any good school where I can play soccer and be near the water. Maybe I'll even go out for crew."

"What if you couldn't go out for both soccer and crew?" Melissa asked. "If you had to choose, which would it be?"

Kirk looked thoughtful, then smiled and glanced at Melissa. "That would be a really tough decision," he said. "But I think I'd pick crew. Of course, I'll probably have to play soccer to get some kind of scholarship, so I hope it doesn't come up."

It was nice talking with Kirk, Melissa decided. The more she learned about him, the more she liked him. Not only was he incredibly cute—Melissa felt like melting every time she looked into his liquid dark eyes—but he was smart and really sweet. Listening to him describe sailing as a kid, she longed to be out on the water with him.

"So what are you interested in—besides me?" Kirk asked with a twinkle in his eye. Melissa blushed a little and laughed. But the question was difficult. Melissa tended to think of herself as pretty ordinary. What could she say that might come close to Kirk's love of sailing or his talent at soccer. Melissa thought about Jill and her obsession with tennis. Jill would have plenty to say in answer to Kirk's question.

"I don't know," Melissa answered thoughtfully. "It seems like I'm interested in everything and nothing. I don't have any great talents or anything."

"What about your job at the flower shop?" Kirk asked. "You seemed pretty involved in working with those flowers when I was there."

"You know, it's funny"—Melissa paused for a moment, thinking about her job—"I complain all the time about working, but when I'm there, doing flower arrangements especially, I really do like it. I've always wanted to be artistic, to make things, but I've never found a way of doing that. Working with flowers is one way. Maybe art is something I'm really interested in, and I just never knew it before!"

Melissa suddenly realized that this was true. She had a real talent for working with flowers; Mr. Grover was always saying that. She felt happy and excited thinking that she'd finally discovered something special about herself. "Maybe when school starts I'll change my schedule so that I can take an art class." The idea excited her.

"Well, I've already seen you at work with a paintbrush, and I was pretty impressed." Kirk laughed, but Melissa felt a little uncomfortable thinking about the day they'd had the paint fight with Matt. She thought about telling Kirk about last night, but she didn't want to spoil things now. On his own, Kirk seemed so much more serious than Matt. She liked the way Kirk talked about himself—sharing stories that seemed to reveal a lot about him. It was so different from Matt's crazy anecdotes about his latest practical jokes.

"You know," Kirk said, interrupting Melissa's thoughts, "I have to tell you, I was really impressed by you the first day we met. The way you handled Matt was great." Melissa wondered what he meant. "Most girl just swoon around him and let him get away with anything," he continued. "But you gave it right back to him. It's terrific to meet someone else who won't let Matt get away with murder." Kirk glanced over at her a little shyly. Melissa smiled, flattered by his comments, proud of the fact that she hadn't let her silly crush on Matt make her act like a total idiot.

"There it is," Kirk said happily as they rounded a bend and came within sight of the lake.

"It looks almost like a small ocean," Melissa said, taking in the enormous lake and incredibly beautiful scenery. The water sparkled under the clear sunny sky. A slight breeze rustled the leaves on the trees. They pulled up in front of a rustic-looking shingled building that was near the water.

"It's a great day for sailing. Let's unload the car and get out there," Kirk said eagerly.

Melissa helped him carry the cooler to the boat, picking the sails up from the boathouse on the way.

They walked down the dock to a slip where a twelve-foot day sailer was tied up. "So, what do you think?" Kirk asked, motioning toward the boat.

"This doesn't look too scary," Melissa said as she climbed into the boat—which was just the right size for two people.

Kirk climbed in after her and wedged the cooler between them. They sat at opposite ends of the boat. Kirk opened the cooler and pulled out a six-pack of soda, offering one to Melissa.

"Thanks," she said, taking a ginger ale. "I'll bet your little sisters are better sailors than I am," she said, laughing. "I hope you're not expecting too much help from me. Paddling a canoe is the closest I've ever come to sailing."

"All you have to do is follow directions when I need an extra pair of hands," he said, throwing a rope in her direction. "Catch!" Melissa caught the rope and began winding it up neatly. "See, you're doing fine," Kirk said with a smile. She watched as he attached the sail to a pin on the mast and then pulled on a rope to hoist the sail up. He repeated the procedure with a smaller sail in the front, then untied the lines that held them to the dock and pushed off.

As Kirk worked, Melissa had the perfect opportunity to admire him. The sun shone on his shiny blond hair, and his crooked smile sent a shiver through her every time he flashed it at her. Melissa was impressed, too, at how quickly he worked, the muscles in his tan arms so strong and lean.

"Here we go!" Kirk said merrily as he let the sail way out to catch the wind. His excitement was catching, and Melissa sat forward expectantly. He moved the stick in his hand—he'd called it a tiller—back and forth, making the boat move from side to side and inch forward. Then a breeze came by and they took off. The wind whipped through his hair and at his windbreaker, making it billow out like the sails. He squinted into the sun and grinned at her. Melissa sat with her back to the wind; she was glad she had worn a sweat shirt.

"You can handle the jib," Kirk said after a few moments, pointing to the little sail at the front of the boat.

"What should I do?" Melissa asked, eager to help out.

"See those two ropes on it? Just pull the one I say to pull, and don't worry." Kirk showed

Melissa which rope to hold. Then they settled into their places on either side of the boat.

For a long time they sailed over the gentle water, not talking, just enjoying the sun and the wind. At first Melissa gripped the rope tightly, afraid to let it move even a little bit. But after a while she found she could tell when to relax and when to keep a firm grip. She scanned the water around them and saw a tiny island nearby. Huge gray rocks jutted out of the water around its shore, and it was covered with short, scrubby trees that seemed to get denser in the center. There was a little sandy slice of beach on one side of the island. It looked like something out of a dream.

"What's that?" Melissa asked, pointing to the island.

"A great place for an afternoon picnic, I'd say," Kirk responded, steering them right toward it. "It's mostly just rocks and some gnarled little trees, but I thought we could pull the boat up onto the beach, eat lunch, and then go for a swim."

As they came closer, Kirk pulled off his jacket and began untying his sneakers. Melissa hesitated, suddenly feeling shy. She wasn't sure she was really the type to wear a skimpy red bikini, and besides, maybe she'd look too fat or too skinny in the wrong places.

"Come on," Kirk said impatiently. Melissa was

impressed again by how great-looking Kirk was, especially in nothing more than swimming trunks. He had a deep tan and his whole body looked muscular and strong. What if he liked girls who looked athletic? Melissa wondered. She'd never had a weight problem, but she could barely manage to stick to the easiest exercise routine.

"Okay, okay," Melissa said. She fumbled with her sandals, trying to stall for time. "Here goes nothing," she mumbled as she pulled her sweat-shirt up over her head. When the shirt was halfway over her head she heard a splash. Yank-ing it the rest of the way off, she looked toward the water. Kirk wasn't even paying attention! Quickly she pulled off her shorts and followed Kirk into the water. It was a little more than waist high.

Pulling the boat to shore was easy, and soon Kirk and Melissa were unpacking the picnic onto a blanket in the warm sun.

"Who's going to eat all this food?" Melissa asked with a gasp, staring at the stuff Kirk was unloading. There was a bag of raw vegeta-bles, two loaves of French bread, cold cuts, a bag of chips, potato salad, cole slaw, and a large pile of brownies. "Are you expecting com-pany?" she asked with a laugh.

"Fresh air and exercise make me hungry," Kirk said seriously. "Besides, we can sit here and eat all afternoon. Let's dig in!" He sat down and sliced one of the loaves of bread lengthwise, then began piling it with cold cuts. Melissa set to work assembling her own sandwich, stuffing half a loaf full of ham and turkey. They happily munched and chatted until they had eaten almost everything.

"I really can't believe we ate all that," Melissa said, laughing and rubbing her stomach. "I'll have to go on a diet for weeks."

"No way," Kirk said, smacking his lips and wiping his mouth with a napkin. "You look great."

"Well . . . right now I need to lie down in the sun and digest that feast," Melissa said blushing. She spread her towel in the warm sand and stretched out. She'd forgotten all about being self-conscious in her bikini. If Kirk preferred girls with athletic builds, Melissa didn't really care. They were together now, and she felt happy and comfortable with him. He spread his own towel next to hers and lay down on his stomach.

"Just don't let me fall asleep here," Kirk said. "I'd hate to wake up and discover the day was over and I had to take you home." He reached over and held Melissa's hand. She squeezed his hand gently and felt a tingle run up her spine. It was wonderful to lie in the warm sun, holding hands, listening to the birds singing. They stayed that way for a long time.

"Okay," Kirk said groggily. "If I don't get up now, I'll fall asleep and you'll be trapped on this island forever." He sat up and shook his head. "Ready for a swim?" he asked.

"Sure," Melissa said as she hopped up from her towel. She felt ready for anything. "Race you to the water," she shouted, then took off before he'd stood up. Still, he almost beat her. They splashed into the water almost at the same moment.

The water was cool, but Melissa plunged in anyway and swam underwater until it was deep enough that she couldn't stand. She came to the surface and floated with her face to the sun, enjoying the feel of tiny waves against her back.

"It's perfect," she said with a sigh. She hadn't felt so happy and relaxed in ages, maybe not all summer.

"A perfect day and the perfect girl to spend it with," Kirk said, swimming over to her. Then he dived underwater and disappeared for a moment. Melissa stared after him, his words ringing in her ears over and over again. *Her*? Kirk Gardener thought that *she* was the perfect girl to spend this wonderful day with? Melissa was sure that this was the happiest day of her life.

Kirk suddenly swam up behind her and

splashed at her. They dodged around in the water, splashing each other, or just floating on their backs and staring at the sky. Finally it was time to get ready to go. Kirk swam quickly back to the little beach. He'd dared her to race him, but she felt too lazy. Slowly she drifted toward the shore. Kirk sat on the beach watching her. When she reached the shallow water Kirk came over to give her a hand, pulling her up onto the sand.

"You look really great," he said, standing close to her, not letting go of her hand. For a moment Melissa thought he would kiss her. Then suddenly he let go of her hand.

"I guess we'd better get going," he said. "It's getting late."

Melissa looked at the sky. The sun wouldn't set for a while, but it was getting late. They packed up the cooler and folded the blankets and towels, then they pushed the little sailboat back into the water. Kirk easily hauled himself back into the boat once they were out deep enough, but Melissa was so worried about tipping the whole boat over that she couldn't manage to pull herself in. Finally, laughing and being half-dragged, Melissa let Kirk help her back into the boat. For a moment he held her in his arms and their eyes met. Then they realized the boat was tipping precariously and she made her way to her seat. Once they started to sail, it got

94

chilly. Melissa pulled on her clothes and held the jib rope tightly, feeling wonderfully happy. She wished they could sail in the little boat forever.

"Well, here we are," Kirk said, sounding subdued as they reached the dock. Melissa helped him tie up the boat and pull down the sails.

"A few more times out and you'll be an expert at this," Kirk said, laughing.

Melissa's heart leapt into her throat. "A few more times," he'd said. He wanted to take her sailing again. Gorgeous, super-popular Kirk Gardener wanted to go out with her again.

Chapter Eight

"What a fabulous day," Melissa said, stretching and settling into her seat as Kirk started up the car. "I can't remember the last time I had such a great time." She smiled broadly and looked at Kirk. He glanced at her and smiled back.

"It was a pretty great day, wasn't it?" Kirk said. "Hey, look," he said, pointing out the window at the view to the west. "It's going to be an incredible sunset tonight. Do you want to find a place to sit and watch it?"

"Sure," Melissa said. She'd be happy to do anything that would make this day last longer. She didn't want to ever go home. Kirk pulled off the highway onto a small side road that led up a hill.

"My family likes to come here for picnics," he said as they came to a stop in the parking lot of a small park. The park was at the top of a high hill, the perfect place to watch a sunset. Near the parking lot was a field of wildflowers.

"Oh, look!" Melissa cried. "Aren't those flowers beautiful." There were daisies and poppies, black-eyed Susans, Queen Anne's lace, cornflowers, and more. The field looked like a patchwork quilt of color. Yellow, orange, and white butterflies flitted above the flowers, and tall grasses swayed gently in the breeze. "Mmm, and smell . . ." Melissa took a deep breath. The air was sweet with the scent of all those flowers.

"Come on," Kirk said. "Let's get out and take a better look."

Kirk and Melissa waded into the field, through the knee-high grasses and flowers. They both began to gather flowers, picking out the ones they thought were prettiest. When they each had a large bunch, Kirk came up to Melissa.

"Here, give me yours." She handed them over, and Kirk added her bunch to his own. Then, with a bow and a flourish, he gave the whole bouquet to her.

"Oh," Melissa cried. "They're beautiful!" She took the bouquet and buried her face in it. It smelled like a summer day. The flowers filled her arms.

"You'll probably want to do something about the arrangement," Kirk said with a grin.

"I'm not going to change them at all," Melissa said. "But I do think I'll hang them up so they'll dry. Then I can keep them forever—a perfect souvenir of today." She smiled at Kirk as she sat down on a rock.

Kirk sat next to her and put his arm around her. They snuggled close together and sat in silence as the sun dipped down into a strip of pink-tinted clouds near the horizon. Golden sunlight streamed out from behind the clouds into the rest of the sky, which was painted yellow and pink and deep violet. All too quickly, the sun was gone and the sky began getting darker. Reluctantly Kirk and Melissa got up and went to the car.

As they drove home, Kirk and Melissa sat silently and listened to the radio, lost in their own thoughts. They'd been driving for a while when Melissa suddenly gasped.

"Oh my gosh!" she said. "I can't believe I forgot to call my parents again."

Kirk looked at her and raised an eyebrow. "Don't worry about it," he said. "We'll stop at the next gas station and you can tell them we're on the way. Besides, it's still early. How about stopping at Pete's on the way home."

"Sure . . . I just hope we don't get the same waitress as last night. Matt really charmed her, but I think she was probably furious after we left." Melissa was about to laugh, thinking about the silly scene at Pete's the night before. Suddenly she realized that Kirk was too quiet. She couldn't believe she had just blurted out that she'd been at Pete's with Matt last night. What a dunce! And she'd been worried about her father giving her away. "I was there with some kids last night," she began lamely. "You know how it gets sometimes—everyone started getting a little rowdy and Matt was there and . . . ."

"Sure, I know exactly how Matt can be," Kirk said abruptly. "I'm just surprised you didn't mention that you'd been out with him last night. No wonder you missed your curfew."

Kirk sounded angry and Melissa felt terrible. But still she didn't really know what he had to be angry about. It wasn't as if she and Kirk were a couple—not yet, anyway. And she still didn't think her night out with Matt really counted as a date. It certainly hadn't been anything like the time she'd spent with Kirk. She wanted to explain to Kirk how she felt, but she couldn't find the right words. She felt tongue-tied and also a little angry. What was he so upset about? What right did he have to treat her like this?

"The only reason I was late last night was because Matt's car broke down," she began. It was really none of Kirk's business, but somehow Melissa felt she had to explain herself to him. Somehow Kirk seemed to be insinuating something had been going on between her and Matt: she wasn't sure what he thought, but she didn't like it.

"I thought you and Matt were friends," she said defensively. "I don't see why it's such a big deal that I had dinner with him and a bunch of other kids. It wasn't anything special. Everybody goes to Pete's all the time."

Melissa crossed her arms over her chest and sank back into her seat. How had the most romantic day of her life suddenly turned into a stupid fight? How could she have been so idiotic as to let it slip about Matt?

The lights of a gas station flooded the highway and Kirk pulled off without saying a word. He stopped the car in front of a row of phone booths.

"Didn't you want to call your parents and let them know you're on the way home?" he asked, sounding depressed.

Melissa sat frozen for a moment longer, then jumped out of the car and made her phone call. When she got back into the car, Kirk had put on a loud tape that made it impossible to talk. As they drove the rest of the way home, she stared out the window, feeling confused. She didn't know whether to be sorry or angry. She wanted to take back the stupid things she'd said. She wanted to talk and laugh with Kirk the rest of the way home, but now he probably hated her. He'd probably never ask her out again. When that thought crossed her mind, tears began to trickle silently down Melissa's cheeks.

"Here we are," Kirk said cordially as they pulled into her driveway. "I hope you had a good time today." He sounded disappointed, but Melissa wasn't sure why. Maybe he wasn't mad, after all. Maybe everything would be okay.

"I've never had a better time in my life," Melissa said with as much enthusiasm as she could muster. "It was an incredible day, thank you." She tried to wipe her tears away nonchalantly before she looked at him, but he didn't seem to notice them.

"Well, I guess I'll see you around," he mumbled, looking down at his hands, which were gripping the steering wheel.

Melissa took the hint to leave. She choked back the new tears that were about to overwhelm her and opened the car door. The idea that he wouldn't even walk her to her door, that they wouldn't share a good-night kiss, made her totally miserable. But she didn't know what to say to change the fact that he had become so withdrawn.

"Thanks again," she said quietly. "It really was a beautiful day. You're a great sailor."

Kirk nodded as if to indicate it was no big thing, and Melissa got out of the car. She walked to the front door even though she wanted to run. Behind her she heard Kirk start his engine. She turned to wave goodbye when she got to the porch, but he had already reached the street and driven away. That was too much. Melissa flew through the door and burst into tears. As she ran upstairs to her room, she heard her mother calling her, but for the moment she just wanted to be alone.

When she got to her room, Melissa threw herself on her bed and sobbed. She kept going over the wonderful day she'd spent with Kirk and the terrible way it had ended. When she remembered the bouquet of wildflowers, she sobbed even harder. She'd been so upset that she'd left them in the car when she'd got out. The thought of the beautiful flowers left to wilt on the backseat of Kirk's car brought on a new wave of tears.

"What on earth is the matter?" Mrs. Darby asked from the doorway to Melissa's room.

"Oh, Mom," Melissa got out between sobs, "I'm such a horrible person."

Mrs. Darby sat next to Melissa on the bed and stroked her hair. "Did you and Kirk have such a terrible time?" her mother asked.

"No, it was wonderful," Melissa cried. "And I ruined everything." Melissa wiped her eyes and sat up, trying to control her tears. She wasn't sure she wanted to tell her mother what had happened, but she needed to tell someone. "We had the most incredible day, sailing and swimming. We had a picnic on this tiny island and on the way home Kirk stopped and picked me this beautiful bouquet of wildflowers. He's just an amazing guy, Mom." Melissa sighed, thinking again about Kirk. "But on the way home I wrecked everything." Melissa sniffed and felt like she was about to cry again.

"How did you 'wreck' everything?" her mother asked with a small smile. "What could you possibly have done?"

"I said something about going out with Matt," Melissa blurted. "Kirk got really mad and I don't even know why."

"I don't see why Kirk should get mad about that," Mrs. Darby said. "Maybe you just misunderstood him. Was he jealous?"

Melissa thought for a moment. Could it be that Kirk was jealous that she'd been out with Matt? Possibly. But it was more likely that he was mad that she'd tried to hide it from him. And there was obviously something between Matt and Kirk that she just didn't understand. Kirk's remarks about Matt had been so cryptic.

"Oh, Mom," Melissa sighed. "I don't know." She sank back onto her pillows and stared at the ceiling, feeling miserable.

"Well, I'm here if you want to talk about it," her mother said.

Melissa wished she could talk about it to Amy or Jill. She couldn't really tell her mother the whole story, not without getting into trouble over going to the lake with Matt, not to mention the fact that Matt's story about being late was a complete lie. What a mess!

"Thanks," Melissa said, "but I think I'll just sleep on it. Maybe tomorrow I'll be able to figure out what's going on."

She didn't believe that for a minute, but what else was there to do? Maybe if she called Kirk tomorrow, she could apologize. She wasn't sure what she'd be apologizing for, but maybe they could straighten things out. Thinking about the blank stare he'd given her before she got out of the car set Melissa to crying all over again. She buried her face in her pillow.

Chapter Nine

When Melissa looked at herself in the mirror the next morning, her eyes were red and swollen from so much crying. Just seeing her reflection made her want to start crying all over again, but she had to get to work. For a change she was looking forward to getting to the flower shop. Maybe if she kept herself busy there, she'd forget about how badly things had ended up last night with Kirk.

When she got to the flower shop, Mr. Grover was on the phone. Sunday was usually a fairly quiet day, but from the sound of his phone call they'd be busy. The caller wanted to confirm flowers for a wedding ceremony to be held that night.

"Do you feel up to doing the bridal bouquet?" Mr. Grover asked Melissa. Obviously her attempt to hide her swollen eyes with makeup hadn't been too effective.

"Sure," Melissa said, forcing a cheerful tone. "It sounds like fun."

She went over the directions for the bouquet with Mr. Grover and then set about collecting the various flowers she'd need. Mr. Grover went to the back room, where he'd have more space to do the table centerpieces and boutonnieres. When Melissa finished the bride's bouquet, she would do bouquets for the three bridesmaids' and the mothers as well.

As she gathered the flowers, wire base, foam, and ribbon she needed to begin her work, Melissa remembered her talk with Kirk yesterday. Just thinking about their discussion of her artistic side made Melissa approach her work today with more seriousness. She looked over each flower carefully before she put it in place, stepping back to view the whole bouquet every once in a while to be sure the ivy fell in just the way she wanted. It made her sad at first to think about talking with Kirk, but as the day wore on and she finished one bouquet after another, she felt better. She had never done such nice flower arrangements.

Melissa was just putting the finishing touches on the last bridesmaid's bouquet—baby's breath and pink rosebuds wrapped in lacy ribbon—when she heard the shop doorbell ring. When she looked up, she was astonished to see Kirk standing in front of the door, waiting for her to look at him before he came into the store.

"Truce?" he said sheepishly, waving something wrapped in white paper. He came in and stood in front of Melissa's counter. "I'm really sorry about last night," he said, looking down at the floor. "I had a great time with you, and I realized this morning that I wasn't very fair. I didn't really have any right to get angry about your going out with Matt." Kirk scowled as he spoke, and he wouldn't look directly at Melissa. He was obviously embarrassed and still upset, but Melissa admired the way he could admit he was wrong.

"It was my fault, too," Melissa said. "I got mad when you got upset and I just couldn't tell you how I felt . . . or how unimportant it was that I'd seen Matt the night before." Melissa looked at Kirk and hoped he'd look into her eyes again, not blankly like he had last night, but with feeling. "What's in there?" she asked, pointing to the large white bundle Kirk was holding.

"I hope there aren't any rules against bringing other flowers into a florist's . . ." He held the bundle out to her.

Melissa quickly pulled the paper away. Inside were her wildflowers. "I thought they'd be all dried out and ugly. I thought you'd just throw them away." Melissa almost felt like crying again. She buried her face in the flowers for a moment to control herself.

"They smell like the field, like yesterday." She smiled at Kirk and held out her hand to him. "Friends again?" she asked. Kirk smiled back, took her hand and shook it, then squeezed it gently before letting go

"What's this?" Mr. Grover's voice came from behind Melissa. He was carrying the finished arrangements all boxed up and ready to be delivered. "Your boyfriend is bringing flowers into my shop from some other florist?" In spite of his words, they could tell he was joking.

Melissa blushed at Mr. Grover's assumption that Kirk was her boyfriend. "We picked these wildflowers yesterday and then I forgot them in Kirk's car. Look, aren't they gorgeous." She held up the bouquet for Mr. Grover to admire.

"Very nice," Mr. Grover said. "Especially since they aren't from Simpson's." He laughed and put his box down on the counter. "You've done a very good job on these," he said, looking over the bouquets Melissa had made.

"Thanks," Melissa said, feeling proud of her work. They were definitely the prettiest bouquets she had ever put together.

"Why don't you two help me load the van and then you can go home. I'm closing early today, since I've got to deliver these flowers and the arrangements I made for inside the church."

After the van was loaded, Kirk and Melissa went back inside to clean off her counter and get her purse, and then all three of them left the shop.

"Have a good time, kids," Mr. Grover said, waving as he drove away.

"He seems to think we've got some sort of date or something," Kirk said with a chuckle.

Melissa blushed. "He means well, but sometimes he jumps to conclusions."

"Well, I think he had the right idea," Kirk said, seeming at ease again. "How about going to Pete's now?"

Melissa smiled happily. That morning she'd been sure he'd never speak to her again. Now here he was, apologizing, bringing her flowers, and offering to take her out. It was almost too good to be true.

"That sounds great," she agreed. "Should we take one car or both drive and meet up there?" She wanted to spend as much time with Kirk as possible, and driving to Pete's with him would give them more time to talk.

"Why don't I drive," Kirk offered. "Then I'll drop you back here to pick up your car on the way home."

Melissa stashed her bouquet in a shady spot in her car and then they were ready to go. On the way to Pete's, Melissa told Kirk how much she had enjoyed her work that day, how their talk about her artistic side had helped her.

"Maybe you just need to start deciding what you really want," Kirk said as they pulled into the restaurant parking lot. "I think your only problem is you can't make up your mind about things." Melissa pondered that as they went inside. "Why don't we sit somewhere a little quiet," Kirk suggested.

"Great idea," Melissa said.

They made their way to a cozy booth in a corner near the back of the restaurant. Melissa noticed that the usual rowdy groups had taken over the center tables and were laughing and talking at full volume. As they made their way through the throng of people, someone called out to Kirk. Melissa recognized him as another soccer player, a guy named Andy Walsh. Melissa had never met him, but according to Jill he was a great guy.

"I just want to stop and say hi," Kirk said, leading her toward their table. "Do you know Andy and Kim?"

"No," Melissa said. "I've never met either of them." But she knew who they were. Andy was a super-popular senior, and Kim was his girlfriend. She was also a senior, one of the smartest math students at Monroe High and vice president of the student council.

Melissa suddenly felt a little nervous. Andy and Kim were part of a crowd that seemed terribly remote to Melissa. Unlike Matt's friends, who were loud and rowdy, Kim and Andy were school leaders. They knew everyone and really seemed to care about their school and the community. And, of course, they also got to run the senior prom, school plays, and pep rallies. There was a grown-up, serious side to their crowd that impressed Melissa at the same time it scared her a little. She was sure Andy and Kim would hardly notice her—after all, Matt's friends weren't as intimidating and they had hardly acknowledged her existence.

"Hi, Melissa," Kim said when Kirk introduced them. "There's room here if you guys want to join us."

"Maybe later, okay?" Kirk replied.

"Great," Kim said. "Why don't you stop by my house for a swim later? A bunch of kids are going to be there."

Melissa was surprised at how nice they were. Both Andy and Kim seemed to want to get to know her. Melissa felt shy and pleased at the same time.

"Thanks, maybe we will," Kirk said. "See

you." Melissa said goodbye and they turned to go.

"They're really nice," Melissa said.

"I'm glad you think so," Kirk said. "They're two of my closest friends." He headed toward a less crowded corner of the restaurant. "So, do you come here a lot?" Kirk asked. "I think I've seen you here before. You looked so familiar when I first met you and I finally figured I must have seen you here."

"Probably," Melissa said, flattered that he'd noticed her before, and surprised. "I come here pretty often with my friends Amy and Jill. We always sit in the same booth." Melissa pointed down the aisle to the booth where she usually sat with her friends. She couldn't help thinking how different it was being here with Kirk compared to how it had been when she'd come here with Matt. Even Kirk's friends seemed different.

"So you were here the other night, huh?" Kirk asked, reading her thoughts. "You must have had a great time if you were with that crowd." He pointed toward the loud group in the middle of the restaurant. Melissa recognized several of the kids she'd been with Friday night, including Susan, who'd given her such a hard time.

"It seemed like a lot more fun at the time," Melissa said, feeling chagrined. "But nobody

112

really had anything to say. It was just a lot of noise—especially about pulling pranks and that kind of thing. It got kind of boring, actually."

"I'll bet I can guess who was doing all the talking—about himself," Kirk said with a smile. "And speak of the devil . . ."

Melissa had her back to the door, but she knew Kirk must have seen Matt come into the restaurant. Melissa worried for a moment that Matt would come over and spoil things. She still wasn't sure how things stood between her and Kirk.

"Oh, never mind," Kirk said, relieved. "He seems to have stopped back there with his friends. We're safe."

Melissa laughed, thinking that she and Kirk were practically hiding out from Matt and his tricks. Only a few days ago the three of them had been goofing around together having a terrific time. Now things seemed more complicated. What would Matt think of her being out with Kirk? Melissa wondered.

"I'd like a cheeseburger, fries, and a Coke," Kirk said, then turned to Melissa. "Are you ready to order?" She'd been staring at the menu, lost in thought, and hadn't realized the waitress was waiting for her.

"Sure," Melissa said. "I'll have a tuna melt and ice tea."

She handed over her menu and glanced at Kirk. He was staring at her with the most incredible expression. He seemed absolutely fascinated. Melissa blushed. Nobody had ever looked at her like that. Self-consciously, she wondered if her eyes still looked puffy. Even if they did, though, Kirk didn't seem to mind.

"I'm glad we could get together today," Kirk said. "After what happened last night, I wanted a chance to talk to you. I wanted to ask you if . . . there's anything going on between you and Matt," he finished in a rush. He paused for a moment and waited for Melissa to respond.

"We're just friends," Melissa said. "We went out that once, but we're not going out or anything." Melissa felt sort of awkward talking about this. She wasn't sure why Kirk wanted to know what had gone on between her and Matt, and she didn't know how much to tell him.

"So, are you dating anybody else?" Kirk asked.

"Not anybody in particular," Melissa answered, feeling a secret thrill race through her. Kirk was trying to find out if she had a boyfriend. Maybe he even wanted to be her boyfriend! Melissa couldn't believe *that*!

"Oh, well . . ." Kirk seemed tongue-tied for a moment. "Then maybe . . ."

Now she was sure she hadn't misinterpreted things. Melissa's heart practically stopped at the thought that Kirk wanted her to be his girlfriend. And right now, that was just what she wanted!

"Hey!" Melissa's heart sank at the sound of Matt's voice right behind her. What timing! "Fancy meeting you two here. You're missing all the action sitting back here in the corner." Matt pulled a chair up to the end of their booth and planted himself on it.

"We were trying to have a conversation," Kirk said, shaking his head. "Not that I'd expect a wild man like you to understand that sort of thing." Kirk managed a smile in Matt's direction, but he obviously wasn't happy about the interruption.

"So, did the intrepid Miss Darby tell you about our adventure on Friday?" Matt asked.

"No," Kirk said. He suddenly looked curious and a little surprised.

"You should have seen her at Highland lake!" Matt whooped with laughter and slapped his knee.

Kirk glanced at Melissa. "You didn't tell me you went out to Highland lake," he said. Obviously, he was disturbed to hear it.

"She was great," Matt went on, oblivious. "Hung right in there with the rest of us. We had to run like crazy to get away from a pack of howling, snarling guard dogs that were hot on our trail, along with three security guards to boot." Matt smiled broadly. He seemed to think Melissa had proved she was one of the gang by her behavior the other night. Matt reached over and hugged Melissa around the shoulders. "I wasn't sure she'd be up for it, but she was."

Melissa was feeling positively mortified. She could tell that Kirk was getting angry. It had been a mistake not to tell him all about Friday night.

"It was pretty funny," she said with a feeble laugh. She looked into Kirk's deep brown eyes and tried to guess what he was thinking, but it was impossible to tell.

"I have to admit," Matt went on despite the deathly silence that had fallen over the table, "I really did think she'd be upset when we forgot all about her curfew."

Oh, no, thought Melissa. *Please, don't say any more.*

"She was sure she'd be grounded for life. Her parents were actually on the porch waiting when we drove up." Matt seemed to take special pleasure in that fact.

"What about your car breaking down?" Kirk asked with a smile.

Melissa knew he wasn't smiling because he thought Matt's story was funny; he was smiling to cover up how angry he was. Why couldn't she say something to make everything okay? Why couldn't Matt just shut up?

"Oh, let's just forget about it, all right?" Melissa said in an effort to change the subject.

"No, I'm really interested to hear how things worked out," Kirk said. There was an edge to his voice and he cast an angry glare at Melissa. "I'll bet Matt really pulled one over on your parents, right?" He was now looking at Matt, who was oblivious to Melissa's dilemma and clearly caught up in telling of yet another great trick he'd played on somebody. It made Melissa uncomfortable to think that her parents were now members of the cast of people in Matt's practical joke stories.

"You'd have been proud of me," Matt said, nudging Kirk. "I sounded as sincere as you." Matt laughed again and Kirk pretended to laugh right along. Melissa considered running out of the restaurant before she heard any more, but she couldn't seem to move.

"So how did you get her out of that mess?" Kirk asked in a tight voice.

"I made up this ridiculous story about the transmission in my car going out on me," Matt said. "It was great. They even offered to let me leave my car there in case there was still something wrong with it!" Matt thought this was the funniest thing of all and proceeded to double over laughing.

Melissa smiled weakly at Kirk, who just looked disappointed.

"Great, Matt, just great," Kirk said with less enthusiasm than Matt might have hoped for. "I just wish I could stick around to hear more, but—" Kirk glanced at his watch—"I've got to run. See you at work tomorrow." Kirk got up, dropped ten dollars on the table, and walked toward the door.

Melissa stared at her plate for a minute. Matt was still jabbering about how stupid her parents were and how funny the whole thing had been.

"Hey, what's the matter?" Matt asked when he finally noticed that Melissa wasn't paying attention to him.

"Umm, nothing." Melissa was trying not to cry. She didn't know what to say. She certainly didn't expect him to understand what had just happened. "I guess Kirk forgot that we came here together in his car. I left my car at work."

"No problem," Matt said cheerfully. "I'm heading home soon and I have to pass right by there. I'll drop you off." He picked some french fries off Kirk's plate and munched them contentedly. "Let's go hang out with the rest of the group and get some ice cream," he said, getting up from his chair. Without looking back he started walking toward the noisy crowd at the center of the room. When he finally noticed she was still sitting at her table, he called to her, "Are you coming?"

"Yeah, just a minute," Melissa said halfheartedly.

She took another bite of her sandwich and picked up her ice tea. After flagging down the waitress and paying the check, she walked over to sit with the other kids. Matt was the center of attention as usual. He wouldn't be leaving any time soon, and Melissa didn't think she could bear to stay much longer. She pulled up a chair and sat down. Too late she noticed Susan at the table next to her.

"Oh, hi," she said just a little too sweetly. "What's your name again? You're the girl Matt brought along the other night, right?" Something about her tone of voice set Melissa off. She didn't like the insinuation that she'd just been tagging along. She'd been as much a part of everything that night as everyone else—for all the good it was doing her now.

"Matt." Melissa waved to get his attention. He was plotting something to do to a friend's car out in the parking lot. "I'm leaving. Gotta go." She smiled as if nothing was wrong, which seemed to satisfy Matt. He waved goodbye and went back to the huddle of guys and their wild plans.

Outside, Melissa got as far as the end of the parking lot before she started to cry. It was a long walk to the flower shop, at least a couple of miles, but she almost felt glad that she had to do it. She felt so terrible, she might as well be stumbling along the busy road. There was no sidewalk and half the time she had to walk in the drainage ditch that ran parallel to the road. She didn't think she'd ever felt worse in her life, and it was all because of boys. Two gorgeous, wonderful, awful boys.

Chapter Ten

By the time Melissa got to her car, she was exhausted. She was also furious with Kirk. No matter how angry he'd been at her, it was hardly fair to leave her stranded. Maybe he wasn't so wonderful, after all. He hadn't even given her a chance to explain. All the way on her long walk she'd gone over things in her head. Maybe she hadn't been totally honest with Kirk, but still, she hadn't meant to deceive him.

Then Melissa remembered how carefully Kirk had been trying to find out if she had a boyfriend. She was sure he'd been about to ask her to go steady with him before Matt had ruined everything. Melissa was angry with both of them, but somehow she was madder at Kirk. Matt hadn't meant to mess everything up—it was an accident. But Kirk deliberately had not waited to hear her side of the story. If only Kirk weren't so serious, if only he'd lighten up and be more like Matt, none of this would have happened.

Melissa opened her car door and slumped into the driver's seat. Then she saw the wildflowers she and Kirk had gathered. They were totally dead after being left in her hot car for so long. Looking at them, Melissa felt a little less angry with Kirk. It really was a mess. Poor Kirk had made such a big effort to patch things up with her . . . sighing with misery, she started her car and headed for home. There was only one thing to do: somehow she had to straighten things out with Kirk. She had to make him see that she wasn't really a liar, that the mess with Matt was just a big misunderstanding. But how?

When she got home, the one thing that could cheer Melissa up was waiting for her—a message that Amy had called and would be calling back at nine o'clock. Melissa went to her room to wait for the call and stared at the ceiling— the same ceiling that Kirk had painted, she couldn't help thinking. She hoped Amy would have some good advice on how to explain everything to him.

"I just had to call when I got your letter," Amy said when she called. "Kirk Gardener and Matt

Warner! I can't believe you're hanging around with them. Tell me everything!"

"Well, a lot's happened since I wrote," Melissa said, suddenly tired of the whole situation. When she'd met the guys, she had seen them more as a way to fill the last boring weeks of summer vacation, maybe even as a ticket to being more popular, but not really as people. Now she could hardly imagine thinking about them except as people, people who were driving her nuts! Starting with the day she stayed home sick to see Kirk and Matt, Melissa explained what had been going on. "So now I don't know what to do," she said finally.

Amy was silent on the other end of the line for a moment. "Wow," she finally said. While Melissa had relayed her story, Amy had kept quiet except for an occasional "really" or "hmmm." Now she said, "What a mess. It sounds to me like you're in way over your head. I can't believe you were actually chased by vicious dogs and security guards. What if they'd had guns?"

Melissa felt even worse now. "Oh, Amy, what am I going to do! I think Kirk is so special. I can't believe how crummy I've been to him. I just didn't expect any of this. And Matt's really funny and I like him, too, but I don't think he'd ever go out with me. I'm not sure he's the type to go out with any one girl. And then there's that creepy Susan. I'm so confused. What should I do?"

"Well, first off, I think you should forget about Matt and concentrate on Kirk. I mean, Matt sounds like he's more trouble than he's worth. Of course, he's a total hunk," Amy conceded.

"Kirk's pretty cute, too," Melissa said, to be fair.

"I know, but Matt's . . . well, he just always looks like he's on the way to a great party, you know?"

Melissa did know. But she wasn't sure that was very important anymore. After spending a little time with Matt's crowd, she didn't know if she really wanted to be part of it. If only she knew what she did want.

The problem was that Melissa still really didn't know Matt. He was so attractive and fun, it was hard not to want to be with him. But the more time Melissa spent with him, the more irresponsible Matt seemed. He was so immature. She found it hard to imagine having a conversation with Matt like the ones she'd had with Kirk. And Matt hadn't tried to find out anything about Melissa's feelings or interests. He just seemed to assume she'd be happy to tag along and admire him—which had been true so far.

Kirk, on the other hand, was open and nice and had a serious side that appealed to Melissa. Talking to him made her think about things, and he seemed to want to understand her, to know her. He was sweet and funny and felt like an honest-to-goodness friend. And when he looked into her eyes, Melissa was sure he felt a special spark, too. If only he wasn't always jumping to conclusions. He never gave Melissa a chance to explain, which only caused her to dig herself deeper into the mess she'd made of things.

"All right, here's my advice," Amy said, getting serious. "Why don't you call Kirk up and explain everything. Say you wanted to tell him about going out with Matt, but you didn't think it was important and it never came up. Tell him you're sorry, and ask him to give you another chance."

"I can't do that!" Melissa cried. "That's the whole problem. I don't think he'd talk to me even if I did call him. Don't forget, he left me stranded, miles away from my car. He must have been really mad to do something that mean." Melissa was beginning to cry. "It's hopeless. I had a chance to go out with the most incredible guy I've ever met, a guy I really like, and I've just wrecked everything."

"Don't give up hope," Amy said soothingly. "We'll think of something. If it's true love and you two were meant to be together, then none of this really matters anyway."

"Oh . . ." Melissa wept into the phone. "Things are worse now than they were before I met Matt and Kirk. Not only am I not popular, but now everyone will think I'm a jerk. At least before, no one knew me."

"Come on, it's not that bad," Amy said. She was beginning to sound annoyed. "Before, all you did was complain about how boring everything was. At least you haven't been bored."

Even Melissa had to laugh at that.

"I guess you're right," she said, sniffing. "But what can I do?"

"I have an idea," Amy said after a pause. "Send him flowers from your shop, something very special, with a card. Write something really sweet and apologetic."

"I don't know . . ." Melissa said uncertainly. "He might just think it was stupid."

"Thanks a lot!" Amy said. "Come on, I bet he'd love it. He sounds very romantic. I think it would work, but you have to do what you think is best. At least it's an idea. Listen, I'm going to have to go soon. My father will kill me when he sees the phone bill."

"I'm sorry," Melissa said. "You're right, at least it's an idea. Besides, what have I got to lose at this point?"

"Nothing," Amy said. "I'll see you in two weeks and I can't wait to find out how things go. I bet you and Kirk will be together by then. I'll keep my fingers crossed for you."

"Thanks, Amy," Melissa said. "By the way, how are things with you and Jeremy?" She suddenly felt selfish for not having asked earlier.

"Wonderful!" Amy said. "I'll tell you more when I see you. Good luck."

After she hung up, Melissa stared at the ceiling and thought about the plan Amy had suggested. Could it work? She might as well give it a try. The more she thought about Kirk, the more she realized she cared about him, and she knew now that she'd hurt him. Even if he changed his mind and didn't want to go out with her, she wanted to apologize.

Melissa spent all the next week at work mulling over her plan. When the shop wasn't busy, she'd pull out the books of flower arrangements and flip through them, trying to get ideas for something to send to Kirk. At first she felt silly even considering sending him flowers. But the more she thought about it, the better the idea seemed. She couldn't forget the talk they'd had about her job, or Kirk's saying that all she needed to do was make up her mind what she wanted and her problems would be solved. More than ever, that seemed to be true. By the end of the week she had made up her mind—she was going to do whatever she could to make Kirk see that she wasn't as awful as she'd seemed and that she really cared about him.

"I'm glad to see you taking such an interest in these books," Mr. Grover said one afternoon; he'd noticed Melissa browsing through yet another book of arrangements. "The more you see in these books, the better your own work will be."

Melissa was finding it interesting to look at all the possible combinations of flowers, but Mr. Grover could never guess her motivation.

"I'm trying to get an idea for a really special arrangement for a friend of mine," Melissa said. Maybe Mr. Grover had some ideas of his own.

"Ah," said Mr. Grover, rubbing his chin. "If you want some free advice from your boss, when I give flowers to someone, I always try to come up with something that shows them I was thinking especially of them. Sometimes I use only their favorite color for the arrangement, or I choose a style that reflects their taste, or I'll even put the flowers in something that reminds me of them."

Melissa thought about Mr. Grover's suggestions and decided she could definitely make use of them. What she needed was a way to show Kirk she cared about him, to say she was sorry for not being honest with him, and to let him know she was thinking about him. She had to make sure he knew she hadn't forgotten the wonderful time they had spent together.

It would have been easy enough to send flowers to Matt, thought Melissa ironically. She could send him a couple of roses with teeth marks in the stems. But Kirk was harder. She thought of buying a model sailboat and filling it with flowers but then decided that would be too corny. Or maybe something to do with soccer. But what? She had to think of something soon.

All week long Melissa had stayed late at work, afraid of getting home before Matt and Kirk finished painting. She wasn't ready to face Kirk, and she didn't want to take any more chances of Matt's coming between them. She missed seeing both of them, but she was also a little relieved not to have to face them for a while. Still, she kept hoping that one or the other of them might drop by the shop to say hello, or that Kirk might call and tell her what he'd been on the verge of saying that awful day at Pete's. But neither of those things happened.

Finally the right idea came to her. Melissa told Mr. Grover that she wanted to stay after work to make the special flower arrangement for a friend, and asked to special-order some flowers.

"This must be a very, very special friend," he said when he saw the list of flowers Melissa needed. "Even with the discount I can give you, this is going to be expensive."

"It doesn't matter," Melissa said. "I have a lot to make up for and this is the only way I could think of to do it." The flowers wouldn't arrive until Sunday, which meant that Melissa had two days to write out a card to send with them.

When she got home from work, Melissa hid herself in her room and filled page after page in her notebook. She had so much she wanted to say to Kirk, but she couldn't seem to find the right words. She tried making up a poem, but that didn't work either.

After what seemed like a hundred tries, she finally wrote a note she was happy with. It read:

Dear Kirk,

I'll never forget the day we went sailing, or the island, or the flowers, or the sunset. It was the best day I have ever spent with anyone.

I can understand why you're angry with me, and I don't expect you to even want to be my friend, but I had to let you know that I'm sorry and I'll always treasure that day.

The next question was how to sign the note. Love, Melissa? Your friend, Melissa? Sincerely, Melissa? Nothing seemed quite right. Finally she wrote just her name.

Sunday when she got to work she was actually excited. She couldn't wait to get started on the flowers for Kirk, but unfortunately it turned out to be a busy day. By the time she was finished with everything that had to be done in the shop, Melissa was exhausted. Nonetheless, she got all her things together, unwrapped the box of flowers that had arrived for her that morning, and set to work. It took hours to get the arrangement done, and it was getting dark out when Melissa finally was satisfied that the flowers looked perfect.

After days of agonizing over what to do, she'd finally settled on an arrangement in a wooden model sailboat—the idea she'd originally thought would be too corny. Instead of sails, Melissa had bedecked the little masts of the boat with delicate white orchids, whose petals shivered and fluttered as if they were real sails blown by an ocean breeze. All around the boat she had arranged a "sea" made up of baby's breath and curled fern fronds. It had come out better than she'd hoped it might, and Melissa felt proud of her efforts as she wrapped the arrangement carefully in cellophane and tied it closed with a bright yellow bow. She carefully nestled the card into the ribbon and stood back to admire the finished product. It was perfect. Kirk would have to be impressed by the hard work that had gone into it. At least Melissa hoped he would be.

Now she had to get the flowers to Kirk without his seeing her. She took the flowers out to her car and drove over to his house. All the lights were off and there weren't any cars in the driveway. Melissa stopped her car across the street and thought for a moment. What if they'd gone away for the week? She was afraid to leave the flowers out on the porch where someone might steal them. But then she remembered Kirk was expected at her house to paint tomorrow, so he'd have to be back before then. She sneaked around the house and left the flowers at the back door.

As Melissa drove home, she crossed her fingers and hoped as hard as she could that Kirk would understand what she was trying to say to him. Now she'd just have to wait.

Chapter Eleven

For the next two days Melissa jumped every time the phone rang. When the shop doorbell jangled, she looked up expectantly, hoping to see Kirk. Every day when she got home from work, she half expected to find a note or something from him left in her room or on the table in the hall. But there was nothing. No phone call, no visit, no note. For all Melissa knew, Kirk had thrown the flowers in the trash and torn her note into a million pieces. By the middle of the week she had given up hope. Then it occurred to her that Kirk might not have gotten the flowers. Maybe someone had stolen them before the Gardeners came home. It was pretty unlikely, but Melissa held on to that possibility because the idea that Kirk just didn't care and didn't want to ever talk to her again was too much for her to bear.

On Wednesday night Melissa was sitting in her room moping. She wished Amy and Jill were back; at least they'd try to cheer her up a little. There was less than a week before school started, but the days stretched for miles ahead of Melissa as she lay on her bed feeling miserable. When her mother knocked on her door, Melissa was glad to have any distraction.

"Hi, Mom," she said listlessly.

"You certainly seem down tonight," Mrs. Darby said.

"Oh, I'm just bored," Melissa lied. "Luckily school starts on Tuesday." She sat up and looked at her mother. "So what's up?" she asked.

"I just wanted to let you know," Mrs. Darby began, "that Dad and I are going to pick Timmy up from camp on Friday. We're going to take him to the Whispering Caves on the way home and stay overnight. We wanted to know if you'd like to stay home and take charge of the house or come with us. We'll be home late on Sunday. What do you think?"

"That sounds great!" Melissa said, perking up. "It would be terrific to have some time to myself." Melissa didn't know what she would do with a whole weekend to herself, especially since her friends still weren't home, but the idea that her parents were willing to let her stay home made her feel incredibly grown-up. They certainly had come a long way since the beginning of the summer when they'd been treating her like a little kid.

"We thought you'd appreciate the time alone," Mrs. Darby said with a smile. "And you've proven how responsible you can be. Just promise me you won't have any wild parties while we're gone." Her mother laughed and so did Melissa. "Oh, and by the way," Mrs. Darby added before she left the room, "the painting's finally done. Did you notice?"

"Ummm, yeah," Melissa said in as indifferent a voice as she could manage. She knew her mother was trying to get some reaction from her about Kirk and Matt. "The house looks great," she said.

"I have to admit I had my doubts about how the work would come out after the day I came home and found the three of you horsing around," Mrs. Darby said. "I was worried those boys would spend more time flirting than working." Melissa blushed. "But they managed to get the job done in time and they did quite well."

After her mother left, Melissa flopped back on her bed and thought about how she could spend her weekend. Just sleeping late, taking long showers and using up all the hot water, and being able to watch whatever she wanted on TV didn't seem like enough. If only Amy and Jill were getting back a few days earlier, she could have them over. Still, it would be fun to be on her own. As she racked her brain for something really special to do with her free time, the phone rang. For a moment she felt the familiar flicker of hope—maybe it was Kirk. Then her hope faded. If he hadn't called by now, why would he ever call?

"Melissa," her mother called from downstairs. "Telephone." Maybe it was Kirk, after all! Melissa leapt off the bed and lunged at her phone.

"Hi," she said, her voice incredibly happy.

"Hi," said an equally happy, friendly voice on the other end of the line.

"Oh," Melissa said. "It's you."

"Gee, thanks," Matt said. "It's great to talk to you, too."

"Sorry," Melissa replied with an easy laugh. "I was expecting someone else. You caught me off guard."

"I like catching people off guard," Matt said, sounding devious.

"I know you do." Melissa felt suddenly glad to talk to him. Matt had managed to cause a lot of trouble, but he was always a lot of fun, too. "So what's up? My mom said you're finished painting."

"Yeah, we are. Actually, I was wondering what had happened to you," Matt said. "It seemed like you just disappeared. I kept expecting you'd turn up at Pete's or something."

"I've just been really busy at work," Melissa said. She wouldn't admit to Matt that she'd been in hiding, afraid to face Kirk's anger and afraid Matt would get her into more hot water. "So what have you been up to?" Melissa expected Matt to have plenty of tales to tell after not talking to him for so long.

"Just the usual," Matt said. "The big event was wrapping Jim's car up with toilet paper the other day at Pete's. It's too bad you didn't stick around for that!" Matt started laughing. "How'd you get home, anyway?"

"I walked," Melissa said. "How did you do that to Jim's car, anyway?" Melissa found it impossible to be angry at Matt no matter how inconsiderate he was. He was such a clown.

"We had a lot of help. You should have seen Jim's face when he walked out and saw it," Matt said with a guffaw. "It was great!" Matt described his crazy antics and soon Melissa felt much better than she had in days. She was actually laughing! It really had been a mistake to avoid Matt all this time, Melissa thought, especially if Kirk was never going to speak to her again.

"So, I was wondering if you want to go to the lake again?" Matt said. "A bunch of us are going on Friday night. This time we'll be ready for the dogs," he added mysteriously.

"Gee," Melissa said. "I don't think so. My parents are going out of town for the weekend, and I'm supposed to take care of things at the house. Besides, I'm not sure I'm ready to face those dogs again." Melissa laughed. She imagined the group taking along big T-bone steaks to throw at the dogs if they came too close. Whatever Matt had in mind would definitely be nutty.

"Hey, that's great!" Matt exclaimed. "Forget the lake. We'll come over to your place and have a party!"

"Ummm . . ." Melissa had a bad feeling about this. She remembered her mother's joke about not having a wild party while they were gone. Matt and his friends *only* had wild parties. "I don't think that's a very good idea," Melissa said, hoping Matt would drop the subject.

"Come on," he said. "It'll be great. The last weekend before school starts? Everybody will be back from their vacations. You can have the greatest party of the summer and it can go on all weekend!"

"It's a great idea," Melissa admitted, trying not to panic at the thought of her house being overrun by Matt's rowdy friends, "but I really can't do it."

"Hey, relax!" Matt said, sensing how nervous Melissa was about the whole idea. "Don't get all worked up about it. It was just an idea. Anyway, I've got to go. Maybe I'll see you at Pete's." Matt said goodbye and hung up, leaving Melissa unsure about whether she'd made the right decision. A tiny voice in Melissa's head reminded her that if she did have a party, she'd score big points in terms of popularity. And Matt was right, it would be one of those parties that everybody came to and talked about for weeks afterward.

But by the time Friday arrived, Melissa had regained her senses and squelched the tiny voice that was rooting for her to let Matt have a party at her house. She helped her parents pack up the car and felt very responsible and proud of herself as she waved goodbye to them that morning. After an uneventful day at work, she decided to go shopping for new school clothes. She had planned to get take-out Chinese food for dinner and treat herself to a feast and a fashion show of her new clothes while she watched cable TV all night. Maybe it didn't compare to having the most talked-about party of the summer, but she was looking forward to it nonetheless.

It was around nine o'clock when the doorbell rang. Melissa had just finished the last of her Moo Goo Gai Pan and was thinking about Kirk, wondering how he could have read her note and not even called to say something. The family room was covered with clothes. She had spent most of the money she'd saved from her job to buy herself a fabulous new wardrobe for school. Jeans and sweaters were draped over the chairs where she'd been laying them out to see how different pieces worked together. She was wearing her bathrobe and the great new boots she'd bought.

Who could that be? Melissa wondered as she peered out the window to get a glimpse of the front door. It was Matt. "Oh, gosh!" she cried out loud. "I'm a mess!" She grabbed a pair of jeans and the blouse she'd been wearing and quickly dressed. The doorbell rang again and Melissa heard Matt pounding on the door and saying insistently, "I know you're in there! Open up."

Melissa hurried to open the door.

"What are you doing here?" she asked Matt.

"I couldn't just let you sit home alone in an empty house on a Friday night," Matt said. He had a mischievous gleam in his gorgeous blue eyes.

"What have you got planned?" Melissa asked suspiciously, not letting him in. "I told you I'm not having a party here tonight."

"Does this look like a party?" Matt asked. He held up his hands to show her they were empty. "I just dropped by to say hi and see if you wanted to change you mind about going to the lake."

"Well . . ." Melissa said, peeking out the door past him. His empty car sat alone in the driveway next to hers. "Come on in." Melissa opened the door so he could join her in the hall. "I really don't feel like going to the lake, though."

"Well, maybe I could hang around for a while?" Matt suggested. "I don't really want to drive out there and hike through the woods by myself, anyway."

"Sure," Melissa said. She was genuinely pleased to have company. "Come on in. Just watch out for the mess." She led him into the family room and swept away a pile of clothes so he could sit down. "Can I get you something to drink?" she asked. "Sorry, I ate everything," she added, noticing Matt looking into the Chinese food containers on the table.

"Too bad," Matt said. "I love spareribs." He shook his head as he held up a bone that had been chewed clean. "You must have been pretty hungry."

Melissa laughed. She had ordered all her favorites and had spent two hours sitting in front of the TV eating.

"Yeah, I'm pretty stuffed," she said. "I'll get some soda." In a minute she was back from the kitchen carrying two glasses of soda and a bag of pretzels. "For you," she said, and tossed the pretzels to Matt.

"Thanks," he said. "They're not as good as spareribs, but beggars can't be choosers. So what's with the clothes?" He looked around at the stacks of clothing all over the room.

"Oh, I went shopping today and I was trying everything on," Melissa said.

"Gee, I'm sorry I missed that, too," Matt said with a smile.

Melissa blushed and got up to gather up the clothes. "I think I'll just dump this stuff in my room," she said as she pulled the last pair of jeans over her arm. "Be back in a second." While she was upstairs, Melissa heard the doorbell ring again.

"I'll get it," Matt shouted.

Melissa suddenly felt a strange fear in the pit of her stomach. She threw the clothes on her bed and raced down the stairs.

"Hey, look who's here!" Matt said with a wide grin. Susan, Jim, and five other kids she didn't know were standing in the hall. "They saw my car," Matt explained.

Everyone poured into the house and headed for the sound of the TV in the family room. "Got any more soda?" Matt asked.

Melissa was paralyzed for a moment. Matt must have planned this all along. She was about to get really angry but then she thought better of it. After all, it was only a few people. She went to the kitchen and found a couple of six-packs of soda, some chips, and some more glasses. Maybe this would be kind of fun.

When she came into the family room, Melissa noticed two more people she didn't know. They were seniors, friends of Matt's. She was about to say something to Matt but got distracted.

"Hey, be careful with that," Melissa said. Jim was fooling around with the stereo, her father's prize possession.

"I just thought we could use some music," Jim said.

"Fine," Melissa said. "I'll take care of it. What do you want to hear?" Suddenly everyone was asking for a different kind of music. No one was happy with the tapes Melissa had.

"I've got some great tapes in my car," Susan offered. When she came back in with the tapes, four more kids followed her.

Melissa had to talk to Matt. The room was getting too crowded. Someone stuck a tape in the machine and suddenly the room was filled with incredibly loud music. Melissa ran over to turn the volume down just as a small table full of glasses fell over. There was a loud crash as the glasses broke and soda spilled everywhere. Someone turned the music back up, and the doorbell rang again. More people came in. Melissa tried to clean up the broken glasses while she looked desperately around the room for Matt. He was nowhere to be seen.

When the glass was picked up, Melissa went to the kitchen to get some towels to clean up the rug.

"Hey, what's going on?" she demanded. A bunch of kids she'd never seen before were taking everything out of the refrigerator.

"We're just getting something to eat," said an indignant girl holding a jar of pickles in one hand and a package of cold cuts in the other.

"Where's the bread?" someone else said.

Melissa didn't know what to do. She had to find Matt. The doorbell rang again. When she left the kitchen, she had to push her way through the family room to get to the spot where the spill was. Someone was standing on it. Melissa threw the towels on the floor in despair just as the phone rang.

"Oh, no!" Melissa gasped, lunging for the phone before some strange boy could answer it. Her parents had said they'd call. "Hello?" Melissa said, trying to cover the receiver a little to muffle the noise of the party.

"Melissa?" It was her father. "What's going on there? I can hardly hear you."

"Sorry, Dad." She searched desperately for an explanation. "The TV's up loud. I was in the kitchen and didn't want to miss anything. Hold on and I'll turn it down." Just then there was a click on the line. "Dad, there's another call, hold on." Melissa pushed the button and the other caller came on the line.

"Hello?" an uncertain voice said.

"Oh!" Melissa said, feeling a sudden wave of relief. It was Kirk! "I'm so glad you called."

"It's really noisy there. Are you having a party?" Kirk sounded confused.

"It's a long story," she began. "Hey, cut it out!" she shouted suddenly. Susan and Jim had started moving the furniture out of the family room into the hall. They were pushing an armchair through the door and about to knock over a porcelain lamp. "Stop!" she yelled too late. There was a terrible crash as the lamp hit the hard floor and shattered.

"Sorry," someone said. Susan and Jim shoved the broken pieces of the lamp out of the way and continued clearing a space where they wanted to dance.

"It's too bright in here anyway!" someone else cried. Everyone laughed as the lights went out. Now there was just enough light to make out people's faces. A group began dancing by Jim and Susan.

"Oh, no," Melissa cried. "What am I going to do?" She'd forgotten she was holding the phone.

"Hello? Melissa? What's going on?" Kirk's voice roused her. "Are you okay?"

"No," she said. "I'm not okay. Matt stopped

by even though I told him not to, and suddenly there are all these people here and they're wrecking the house and I can't get them to leave and my parents are on the phone—" Melissa stopped short. "Oh, gosh, I forgot all about them! I have to go, Kirk. I'm really sorry." Melissa hung up the phone feeling totally horrible. Quickly she unplugged it and then ran to the kitchen and unplugged that phone. She could hear the phone upstairs ringing as she ran toward the steps. It must be her parents calling back.

"Hello," she said, trying not to sound too out of breath. She'd closed the door to her room so her parents wouldn't hear the noise from the party.

"Melissa? What's going on?" Her father sounded a little annoyed.

"I'm sorry, Dad," she said. "That was Kirk who called and I just forgot you were on the other line." At least she could tell the truth for a change.

"Oh, I'm glad you two are talking," he said in a more relaxed voice. "I know you like him. We just wanted to say hi and see how everything was."

"Everything's fine, Dad," Melissa said, hoping she sounded more calm than she felt. "Tell Timmy hello for me. I want to get back to see the end of that movie, okay?"

"Have a good time," her father said. "We'll see you on Sunday."

"I love you," Melissa said. She felt terribly lonely suddenly. She held the phone in her hand for a minute before hanging it up. The noise downstairs seemed to be growing louder, if that was possible. She dreaded facing the catastrophe that awaited her there, but somehow she had to break up the party and try to repair the damage that had already been done. But where was Matt?

147

Chapter Twelve

"Matt! Matt, where are you?" Melissa shouted at the top of her lungs as she shoved her way through the crowd. *"Matt!"* It was no use. Nobody could hear her over the din of music and conversations being yelled from one end of the room to the other. She'd just have to make her way through the house until she found him. As she pushed from one room to another, she tried to rescue things that were in danger of being destroyed. She flipped the light switches back on, hoping the light would calm everyone down or give them the message to leave.

"There must be fifty people here, at least," she said to herself, slumping against a wall for a moment. She was beginning to think there was no way to get them to leave. She imagined them all still there when her parents came home on Sunday afternoon. By then the house would be in ruins.

"Great party, huh?" said a guy Melissa had never met.

"Yeah, great," she replied sarcastically. She turned and began wading through the bodies to get to the kitchen.

Finally she saw him. Matt was standing in a relatively quiet corner of the kitchen talking to a bunch of girls who looked like freshmen and sophomores. They giggled and smiled adoringly at him. Matt was obviously having a great time.

"Excuse me, Matt," said Melissa, stepping into the middle of the circle, "but we need to talk." She was so angry now that none of Matt's charm, not those twinkling blue eyes or that dazzling smile, could affect her.

"What's up?" he asked innocently. "Didn't I tell you this would be the greatest party of the summer?" He smiled and looked around as if he were proud of having arranged such a wonderful party.

"Great? You think this is great?" Melissa was practically screaming. "I don't even know who these people are! They're trashing my parents' house and I want them out of here. *Now!*"

Matt looked surprised. "Whoa, hold on. I

thought you'd have fun once the party got started, honest. I just figured you needed a little convincing, that's all." Matt looked totally baffled. "I can't just tell everyone to *leave*."

Melissa couldn't believe it. Obviously Matt wouldn't help her out of this mess. He just didn't seem to understand. He really believed it was a great party.

"Thanks a lot, Matt," she said before she turned and left. She stalked out of the kitchen, fuming. How was she going to get rid of all these people?

Melissa went into the family room and was shocked to see the crowd thinning out. People seemed to be leaving in droves, and someone had actually shut off the music.

"Hey, what's going on?" Melissa asked a girl who was picking up her purse and shoes to leave. "Where's everyone going?"

"Didn't you hear? There's a big party over at the Warners'. There's going to be swimming and a *live band*, and they're going to have pizza at midnight!" The girl hurried off to join a large group of kids waiting at the front door.

"A party at the Warners'?" Melissa asked to no one in particular. "Matt Warner's?" Something strange was going on here. Within ten minutes almost everyone was gone. Melissa walked through the house in shock at the mess they'd left behind. She'd have to work like a dog to clean the place up before Sunday, and she'd have to go shopping for a new lamp and new glasses. It seemed like an awful lot had been broken. Still, it could have been a lot worse. At least no one had ventured up the stairs. The destruction had pretty much contained itself in the living room. Melissa went back into the kitchen, the only room where anyone was still left.

"Where is everybody?" wondered a girl who had just noticed how empty the place had suddenly become.

"They went to the big party at the Warners'," Melissa said, smiling. Matt looked up at the sound of his name. There were only a few people in the kitchen. Melissa told the girl what she had heard about the other party, and the girl and her friends, who seemed to be all the people left at the party except Matt and Melissa, suddenly hurried out.

"What was that you said about a party at my house?" Matt asked incredulously.

"I just told her what someone else told me, Matt." Melissa shrugged. "I don't know what's going on, but apparently you're having a big party with a band, pizza at midnight, and even swimming in your pool." Melissa couldn't help laughing at the expression on Matt's face. He looked astonished, angry, and confused.

"That was a really crummy thing to do," he said, glaring at her.

"I told you," she said, "it wasn't my idea. Looks like somebody is playing a joke on you for a change! I only wish I'd thought of it." Melissa sat down in a chair and looked back at Matt. "I guess you'd better go home and see how the party's going." Matt didn't say another word but just stormed out. A moment later she heard his car peeling out of the driveway.

Melissa sat at the table with her head in her hands for what seemed like an eternity. Slowly she realized she had to get to work repairing the damage his little prank had done to the house.

The kitchen seemed a logical place to start cleaning up. It was also the least messy room; nothing in it had been broken. Melissa got out a giant trash bag and started filling it with paper plates of half-eaten food, paper cups, soda cans, and other junk that people had left behind. She was amazed at the amount of food that had been wasted. Tomorrow she'd have to go shopping to restock the kitchen. There went the rest of the money she'd saved from her job, she thought glumly. If only she could make Matt pay for the food and the broken stuff. He was really to blame. But—her thoughts were interrupted by the doorbell.

"Oh, no," Melissa groaned. They wouldn't come back, would they? She was afraid to answer the door, so she sneaked to the window first and looked out. She couldn't believe her eyes.

"Kirk!" she called, unable to contain her happiness at seeing him. "What are you doing here?" she asked as she opened the door and ushered him in.

"I thought you might need a little help cleaning up," he said, smiling. "I'm sorry I couldn't find you when I came in before, but it seemed like it was more important to clear the place out fast than to say hi."

"What do you mean 'before'?" Melissa asked. "You were here before? When?" Then it dawned on Melissa. "It was you! You started the rumor about the party at Matt's! Oh, you're fantastic!" Melissa jumped up to hug him around the neck without thinking about it. He hugged her back and then gently pushed her away so that he could look at her.

"I was really confused and worried when you hung up on me," Kirk said. "And then I realized what must have happened. Matt found out your parents were away, right?" Melissa nodded. "And then he just dropped by . . . and then so did a bunch of his friends?"

"That's exactly what happened," Melissa said. "Even after I told him that I absolutely didn't want to have a party here when my parents were gone. He was so mean. I couldn't believe it."

"He's pulled stunts like that on friends before," Kirk said. "Nothing as bad as this, though. Anyway, I think tonight should cure him of it." Kirk started to laugh. "I actually drove people over to his house!"

"But won't his parents just kick everyone out?" Melissa asked.

"Probably, but it won't matter—the damage will be done. Someone's bound to say enough to get Matt in trouble. I don't think even Matt will be able to talk his way out of this one."

Melissa was amazed. "I had no idea he could be such a creep," she said. "I thought he was just a funny guy who liked to have a good time."

"Basically he's a good guy. He just forgets to think about other people's feelings sometimes. He didn't mean to wreck your house. He probably just didn't even think about it."

"Well, I guess I'd better get to work cleaning this place up," Melissa said.

She and Kirk went through the rooms picking up garbage. For a long time they didn't talk. Kirk had put a tape on the stereo and they just worked quietly, listening to the music. Melissa wanted to ask Kirk a million questions, like why hadn't he called her sooner? Had he gotten the flowers? What did he think of her? But she didn't want to spoil the mood between them, not yet, anyway.

"This is going to take hours," Kirk said, surveying the disaster area that had been the Darbys' living room. "I think we should call it a night and get a fresh start in the morning." Kirk collapsed into the armchair that was still sitting in the hallway. "How about you? You must be exhausted." They'd worked for two hours. The garbage was gone and most of the mess was straightened up, but the floors and rugs were filthy, there was a mile-high pile of dishes in the kitchen, and some of the furniture still needed to be moved.

"I guess you're right," Melissa said. She'd have been happy to stay up all night cleaning just to be with Kirk, but she had to agree with him. "I really am tired."

"I'll be back around ten, okay?" Kirk said. "I'll help you clean up the rest of this mess and then maybe we can go out somewhere."

"There's a lot I want to talk to you about," he explained when Melissa looked surprised. "But I'm just too beat right now." Kirk yawned and stretched, then rubbed his eyes. He was silent for a moment, then shoved himself back on his feet. He took the big bag of garbage Melissa was holding. "I'll put this out on my way," he said, gazing into Melissa's eyes. When he smiled at Melissa, she had to smile back.

"Thank you so much, for everything," she said as she led him to the porch. They stood looking into each other's eyes for a moment, then Kirk headed for his car.

Melissa stood on the porch and stared at the starry sky. She felt so tired from all the work, but her head was whirling with emotions. She was thrilled that Kirk had come to help her out. And she was dying to know what he wanted to say to her. Then there was Matt. She was so disappointed in him. Everyone just seemed to accept the way he was, but Melissa knew now that she never could. Finally she sighed and turned to go inside. She locked up and turned off the lights, then slowly climbed the stairs. She was so exhausted that she didn't even bother to move the pile of new clothes that she'd thrown across her bed. She just lay down beside them and slept.

Melissa was sound asleep when the doorbell rang the next morning. She heard it in her dreams and slowly realized it was real.

"Coming," she mumbled as she pulled on her bathrobe and staggered down the stairs. She opened the door to see Kirk smiling down at her.

"Good morning," he said cheerfully. "Can I come in?"

"Oh, sure," Melissa said, still groggy. "I'm sorry, I guess I overslept. I'll just run upstairs and—"

"Take your time," Kirk said. "You look like you need a shower to wake you up."

Melissa dragged herself up the stairs and into the bathroom. Once she got in the shower, she began to feel better. Finally awake, she got out and dressed quickly in old jeans and a T-shirt, then went downstairs to see Kirk.

"I was hoping to find something to eat," Kirk said. He was sitting at the kitchen table with yesterday's newspaper. "But they really cleaned you out last night. There's nothing left."

"Ugh," Melissa said. "I know. I'm planning to spend the afternoon at the grocery store." She opened the refrigerator and peered inside. "Hey, I found some eggs. How about an omelet?"

"That would be great," Kirk said with an appreciative smile.

Melissa quickly made the eggs and soon set two plates on the table.

"So, um, last night you said that you wanted to talk to me," she said after they'd been eating in silence for a while.

"Um, yeah. I've been trying all this time to think of what to say," Kirk said. "I felt awful that day in Pete's. I was beginning to think that you and Matt were in league together, that you

157

were pulling some joke on me. I guess I couldn't take it. I really care about you a lot, Melissa."

Kirk stopped and stared at his plate. "I just couldn't figure you out. I thought you liked me, too, but then Matt kept popping up and I thought maybe you weren't interested in anything more serious than goofing around and playing jokes." He looked at Melissa. Now was the time for her to be honest, too.

"I guess I wasn't sure what I wanted either," said Melissa, looking directly at Kirk. "Until I thought you'd never speak to me again. Then I realized how much I liked you. I just didn't know what to do about it. So I sent you the flowers, and you never . . ."

"I know," Kirk looked down at the table. "I feel awful that I didn't call right away."

"Then you did get them?"

"Yes. They were the most beautiful flowers I've ever seen. No one's ever done anything like that for me." He was silent for a moment, thinking. "I guess I didn't know what to say after that—how to apologize. I was so mean to you—stranding you at Pete's and all—and then you send me flowers. I felt like such a rotten person."

Neither of them spoke for a while.

"I'm glad you liked them," Melissa finally said quietly. "But I've been miserable for days thinking you'd gotten the flowers and the note and just never wanted to have anything more to do with me."

Kirk toyed with a button on his shirt. "I wanted to call. I wanted to see you and pick up where I left off at Pete's that day . . ." His voice trailed away. "I don't know. Maybe we should talk about this later," he said. "Why don't we get to work."

Melissa sighed. Obviously Kirk liked her, but now he seemed afraid to tell her how he felt. *I'll just have to be patient, that's all,* she vowed.

"Where do you want to start?" Kirk asked, looking around. There was still a lot to do.

"How about the dishes? Then the kitchen will be back to normal." Melissa filled the sink with hot, soapy water and started to wash things that wouldn't fit into the dishwasher while Kirk loaded up the machine.

"I think we're going to have to fill this thing up a few times," he said. "How about some music?" She nodded and he went into the other room and put on her favorite tape, Tracy Chapman. It definitely helped keep the pace going. Finally the last dish was washed and put away. Not it was time to tackle the floors.

Melissa got out buckets and mops, the vacuum cleaner, and some rug shampoo. She and Kirk spent most of the day hard at work trying to get the stains out of the rugs and get the floors clean. They put on dance music and Kirk began dancing with his mop. Melissa joined in, doing a terrible tango across the room. When Kirk saw her, he cracked up, which made Melissa laugh, too. Finally they had to stop because they were laughing so hard.

"I never thought I'd have so much fun cleaning the house," Melissa gasped, out of breath from laughing and dancing and mopping.

"Me neither," Kirk laughed again.

By three o'clock they'd finished and were both exhausted.

"Thanks, Kirk," Melissa said, turning serious. "You're the best friend in the world to help me out like this. Now I guess I'd better go shopping before the stores close. I've still got to get a lamp and some glasses, and a lot of food." Melissa groaned and fell back onto the couch. "But first I'd really like to take a nap."

Kirk laughed and walked over to stand beside her. He held out a hand to help her up.

"Come on," he said. "I'll go with you. It'll go quicker that way. And then maybe we can go to a movie or something." His smile was so sweet and his eyes were so kind and full of fun, Melissa wanted to throw her arms around him.

"You're terrific," she said sincerely, taking his hand. "You've turned what should have been the greatest mess of my life into an incredibly fun day." She smiled and got up. "Why don't we both change and you can meet me back here in half an hour."

Kirk nodded, and Melissa went upstairs to wash her face and brush her hair. She'd kept it braided and out of the way while they were cleaning, but now she wanted to look her best. She brushed and brushed her long hair until it was soft and full. It was wavy, too, from being braided. Then she changed into a pretty white sundress and put on a little of the new makeup she'd bought but never worn. Finally she added turquoise earrings to match her eyeshadow. Then she slipped on her fancy sandals and spritzed herself with perfume, and was ready to go.

"You look beautiful," Kirk said when she met him at the door a little while later. He had changed out of his cut-offs and grungy T-shirt and was wearing tailored white pants and a pale blue button-down shirt.

"So do you," Melissa giggled. He held his hand out to her and they walked to his car.

Two hours later, Melissa slumped over the hood of Kirk's car with an armload of grocery bags. "Finally," she sighed. "We're finished." They loaded up the car and got in. "Boy, am I tired."

"Me, too," Kirk agreed. "And starving. Want to get some dinner?"

"Mmm," Melissa said. "That sounds like a good idea. Where shall we eat?"

"How about Pete's?" Kirk said with a mischievous glint in his eye.

"I don't know." Melissa laughed. "Last time we went to Pete's, things didn't work out so well. Besides, I'm much too tired to walk home tonight." It felt good to be able to joke about that horrible day.

"I'm really sorry about that," Kirk said seriously. "You must have thought I was a real jerk for stranding you like that, no matter how mad I was." He seemed genuinely sorry.

"It wasn't your finest moment," Melissa said, not caring about that day at all now. "But I still don't understand why you got so angry. I mean, I know I wasn't honest with you and that was awful, but you didn't even give me a chance to explain anything. It was kind of confusing."

"I wanted to tell you earlier today, but . . ." Kirk paused. The atmosphere in the car seemed heavy suddenly. "You see . . . Matt and I have a long history of being interested in the same girls." Kirk stared at the road and gripped the steering wheel tightly. He seemed uncomfortable talking about this. "The last girl I went out with, almost a year ago, was someone I thought I knew pretty well. I liked her a lot and I thought we had something special. We'd been dating about five months when I found out she and

Matt had been going out all that time. It turned out she didn't really care for me at all, and it was thanks to one of Matt's stupid jokes that I found out about the whole thing."

"That's terrible," Melissa said. "No wonder you got so mad." Suddenly it all made sense. "But you and Matt are still friends, aren't you?"

"He's not the kind of friend I'd trust with my deepest secrets," Kirk said with a wry smile, "but he's an okay guy if you don't expect much from him. Besides, it was the girl who was keeping things secret, not Matt. As far as Matt was concerned, the whole thing was no big deal. He stopped seeing her, too."

"It sounds like a pretty depressing situation," Melissa said.

"It was," Kirk answered. "Anyway, I was afraid it was happening all over again with you. I'm really sorry."

"That's okay," Melissa said quietly. Then in a lighter voice she said, "So, what about getting some dinner?"

"How about this," Kirk said, seeming relieved to get off the subject of Matt, "let's get take-out from Pete's and eat it at your house. We've got to get your groceries back home anyway."

"That sounds great," Melissa agreed. They drove on to Pete's and picked up burgers and fries and headed back to her house.

"This was a great idea," Melissa said, finishing the last of her fries as they sat cozily in front of the television set.

"Yeah, it was," Kirk agreed. "But I'd better get going. I'm exhausted. You really know how to put a guy to work." He laughed. "My parents will probably want me to do all the yard work tomorrow, so I'd better get home and get some sleep." He stretched and yawned. Melissa got up and walked him to the front door.

"I'm glad we finally talked about things," she said. Still, she felt there was something important they hadn't talked about—the thing Kirk had almost talked about that day at Pete's. Melissa hoped he wouldn't leave until he'd said what he'd almost said then.

"Thanks again for helping me with all this," she added, feeling grateful for his help and happy that he'd spent the day with her. She also felt shy and expectant. Something was going to happen, she knew it. Maybe he would finally kiss her. Maybe he would ask her what he'd started to ask her that day at Pete's.

"It's late," Kirk said, looking at his watch. He seemed nervous suddenly. "I should go home."

Melissa led him out to the porch. They stood there for a long time, holding hands and looking into each other's eyes.

"You look like you want to say something," Melissa said, trying to make it easier for him.

She knew Kirk was hesitant because he had been hurt before.

"Melissa," he began, "I really care about you . . . a lot . . . and I think, especially after today, that you care about me, too. So, I was thinking . . ."

"I was thinking something, too," Melissa said when Kirk paused nervously. "I was hoping we could start going out—"

"Oh, Melissa," Kirk said as he bent down to kiss her. He pulled her toward him and wrapped his arms tightly around her and their lips finally met. It was a soft, gentle, wonderful kiss, just as she'd imagined it would be. They kissed for a long time, and then just stood in the cool night air, holding each other.

"I'm sorry about everything that happened before," Melissa said quietly. "I was so confused."

"Me, too," Kirk said, giving her a squeeze.

"I have a friend who says that when it's true love, none of that other stuff matters."

"Your friend must be right," Kirk said. He smiled at her. "But I guess I'd better get home." They kissed again, briefly, and then headed for his car.

"I'll call you tomorrow to see how things go with your parents when you tell them about the party," Kirk said.

"Thanks," Melissa said. On impulse, she leaned through the window and gave him a quick kiss. Feeling slightly dazed, she stood on the porch and watched him leave. When she went back into the house, she felt as if she were floating. She thought how exciting it would be to tell Jill and Amy about this day as she got ready for bed. It was hard to believe that only three weeks ago she had been so unhappy. It was hard to believe she hadn't expected to fall in love—but it had happened anyway. Despite everything, it had happened.

Melissa slipped into bed and dreamed of Kirk's deep brown smiling eyes, his strong arms holding her, and his lips against hers.

We hope you enjoyed reading this book. If you would like to receive further information about available titles in the Bantam series, just write to the address below, with your name and address: Kim Prior, Bantam Books, 61–63 Uxbridge Road, Ealing, London W5 5SA.

If you live in Australia or New Zealand and would like more information about the series, please write to:

Sally Porter
Transworld Publishers
(Australia) Pty Ltd
15–23 Helles Avenue
Moorebank
NSW 2170
AUSTRALIA

Kiri Martin
Transworld Publishers (NZ) Ltd
Cnr. Moselle and Waipareira
Avenues
Henderson
Auckland
NEW ZEALAND

All Bantam and Young Adult books are available at your bookshop or newsagent, or can be ordered at the following address: Corgi/Bantam Books, Cash Sales Department, PO Box 11, Falmouth, Cornwall, TR10 9EN.

Please list the title(s) you would like, and send together with a cheque or postal order. You should allow for the cost of book(s) plus postage and packing charges as follows:
80p for one book
£1.00 for two books
£1.20 for three books
£1.40 for four books
Five or more books free.

Please note that payment must be made in pounds sterling; other currencies are unacceptable.

(The above applies to readers in the UK and Republic of Ireland only)

BFPO customers, please allow for the cost of the book(s) plus the following for postage and packing: 80p for the first book, and 20p for each additional copy.

Overseas customers, please allow £1.50 for postage and packing for the first book, £1.00 for the second book, and 30p for each subsequent title ordered.

First love . . . first kiss!

A terrific series that focuses firmly on that most important moment in any girl's life – falling in love for the very first time ever.

Available from wherever Bantam paperbacks are sold!

SILVER SKATES

by Barbara J Mumma

To become a top figure skater, you need talent, determination and dedication. Just as important however, as four young hopefuls Claire, Whitney, Cindi and Katie found out, are good friends!

A stunning series starring young skaters – for every teenager who has ever dreamed of gliding across the ice in the arms of the boy they love.

Available wherever Bantam paperbacks are sold.

1. BREAKING THE ICE
2. WINNERS WALTZ
3. FACE THE MUSIC
4. TWO TO TANGO